Vengeance is Mine

by

Michael Landolfi

"The man who has lost everything is capable of anything."

—Clyde Shelton, from the movie *Law Abiding Citizen*

    Why did Capote spend half a decade writing *In Cold Blood*?

    Were his words meant to satiate our desire to feed on others' misfortune or to alert us to the cruelty, the macabre minds and the monsters running loose in the world?

    Was he so astonished by the randomness and brutality of the crime that he simply had to tell the story?

    Or, was he just trying to make a buck?

1

The End (Part I)

"Do you have any last words?" asked the warden.

Martin Cochran blinked his eyes at Warden William Phillips. He was calm and controlled. He took in a slow, deep breath and whispered, "Yes I do, warden."

The curtain that hung between the witnesses and the death chamber had just been opened. Now, the audience had a full view of the condemned prisoner. Worn, but sturdy, brown leather straps ensured his cooperation. He was connected to IV lines and a cardiac monitor. Plastic IV bags dripped clear solutions into both arms. Soon, one would deliver death. The electrocardiograph recorded each heart beat as it occurred. Soon, it would announce his death. But, for now, a steady beep, beep, beep resounded throughout the death chamber. The killer's pulse was sixty-four, a normal resting heart rate.

The event was being recorded, and the camera operator zoomed in on the condemned man's face. On the monitor, I could see that his eyes had closed. He seemed to be seriously contemplating how to best express his deathbed thoughts, how to eloquently convey his final message. All the people in the audience held their breath and, in silence, awaited the condemned man's final words. Time stopped.

I imagined that the chaplain and the victim's family members wished for a heartfelt apology and a request for forgiveness. And I bet that Dr. Martin Cochran's ex-wife, Cindy, prayed that the potassium chloride solution that stops the heart, or the paralyzing drug, would be released *now* — prior to the sedative — killing him painfully before he could utter another word.

I had no idea what Cochran might say, but I figured it would be interesting. The whole bizarre case had captured my full attention from the moment I first learned of it.

He inhaled deeply again and struggled with both leather wrist restraints. He strained against the sturdy chest strap, but could only crane his neck. Then, while glaring at those gathered to observe his execution, Cochran flashed a wicked smile and softly continued, ". . . I would just like to say, sir . . ."

And he quoted *The Bible* . . .

2

The Beginning

**My name is Pierre Fontaine. I used to be a reporter for
the *Dallas Daily* and I *used* to be married.** But investigating the intriguing case of Dr. Martin Cochran cost me
that job *and* finished off my marriage. Why I was so obsessed with a convicted murderer, a death row inmate, a
demon who tortured his wife, I'm not certain. Could it
have been a morbid fascination with a life that was
about to end and the evil deeds that led the former doctor to the death chamber? Was I simply bored with the
subjects that I had been reporting on lately? *Or* was it
Kismet? Good questions.

At least part of the answer lay in the fact that my life
had taken a sad turn for the worse in the last eighteen
months, and the economy's nosedive had a lot to do
with that.

First, newspaper subscriptions and readership had
plummeted — people still wanted the news, but mostly
for free over the internet — and so, the *Dallas Daily* was
struggling for survival. In the dog-eat-dog, news-media
world, the papers are losing the battle. My job was on
the line as were those of many fellow employees.

Secondly, the collapse of the housing market had
crippled my wife Kelly's real estate business. That event
pushed our finances and our vowed union to the very
edge of an "irreconcilable abyss."

Kelly had been a successful real estate agent, but
during the past few months her had income dropped to

almost nil, along with our bank balance. She was working hard to sell properties, but no one was in the market—the banks weren't loaning and the prices were too high. She became increasingly depressed and angry.

Our marriage had been on the skids for six years, ever since the car wreck in which Kelly had lost the twins before they were born—*and* it was "my fault." Here's the short version: Kelly went into labor around noon and called her obstetrician. The doctor said to wait until the contractions were about five or six minutes apart and then come to the hospital.

We headed to the hospital at 7:30 p.m., and along the way drove through a huge thunderstorm. Visibility was almost zero, as torrential rain and golf ball-sized hail pummeled the windshield. When a semi sped past, I swerved a bit too much, hydroplaned, and wrecked in a deep ditch, the car flipped upside down. Kelly and I were both knocked unconscious and held in place by our seatbelts. I regained my senses before my wife did, but couldn't free myself or her.

Hours later, we were rescued and taken to the hospital, but by then the babies were dead. Kelly still hasn't forgiven me for the accident, and our relationship has never been the same since it occurred.

The more dismal her business became, the worse Kelly felt. She started smoking again and drank too much. I became her whipping boy.

The last, but probably not the least, factor contributing to my decline is that I have lost much of the zeal that I used to have for my job. Of late, my assignments have been chosen for me. And as a result my writing has suffered.

For a number of years, I was well respected and had delivered many top-notch stories. My articles were often on the front page, and my in-depth reporting earned me two Pulitzer Prize nominations (unfortunately, I never received an actual award). In 2005, I was nosed out by the folks at the *Star-Ledger* for their great job reporting on the New Jersey governor who admitted to being gay and cheating on his wife with a male lover. Then, in 2006, I was nominated again. That time, I reported on the train bombs in Mumbai that killed two hundred people and wounded many more, but the *Times-Picayune* trumped the field with its excellent coverage of the Katrina disaster.

Sadly, in the spring of 2007, my editor started assigning topics. Some of the junior reporters were used to this, but I wasn't. As a consequence, I've struggled and I guess it's shown.

I realize that the paper is in stiff competition with TV news channels, the Internet, You Tube, and all sorts of instant media sources. And *they're* all competing with short attention spans, rising prices, and plummeting incomes. I know they all must report the same major stories — each one attempting to find some twist to grab attention and secure as much of the market as possible. But I believe that with freedom comes imagination and sometimes artistic triumph. Corporate America is all about maximizing efficiency and minimizing waste — therefore assignments make sense to the big wigs. But I found most of them tedious and boring.

So, the impending execution of Dr. Martin Cochran immediately grabbed my attention. I felt like it could be *the* story that would put my career back on track — my professional salvation. And maybe, if things went well, it might help resurrect my marriage.

I first heard about Martin Cochran while I was riding in a taxi from LaGuardia airport to my hotel room at the Hilton Garden Inn. I was attempting to read the *Times*, but couldn't quite focus. NPR's "All Things Considered" was playing loudly on the radio and my ears caught snippets of the story. Finally, the Pakistani cabbie broke in and stated in staccato English, "They're going to execute that crazy doctor on Friday, you know."

"What?" I answered. I could barely understand him.

"You know, that crazy doctor who cut up his wife."

"No, I *don't* know. Who are you talking about?"

I put down the paper, and Ahmer turned down the radio. Then, while snaking through crushing, stop-and-go, Queens traffic, and looking over his shoulder every three seconds, he related the story while I tried to follow his deplorable diction.

The short version of Ahmer's long-winded tale was that a dozen years ago a young doctor and former Marine, Cochran, caught his wife cheating on him. During a nasty divorce, he lost everything—*including* his sanity. After the divorce, he went berserk and got revenge by "butchering" his ex-wife and murdering the private eye who had worked for him. Now, he was scheduled to be executed by the state of South Carolina on the first of July—in just six days.

I was surprised that I'd never heard of the story. And it seemed like it might feather in nicely with my present task. Over the past two weeks I'd been gathering information for a story on divorces of military personnel. My assignment was to compare the divorce rates of combatants and non-combatants, and to detail the precipitating factors and outcomes. I was fairly interested in the subject, since my father had been a Korean War veteran and my parents' marriage ended in divorce when I was seventeen.

I became even more interested in Dr. Martin Cochran when I learned that he'd been a decorated Force Recon Marine in the Vietnam War. And since his divorce ended in mayhem and murder, it was a terrific example of negative divorce outcomes.

I discovered that and a lot more when I got to my hotel room and fired up my laptop. First, I pulled up the "All Things Considered" broadcast notes and read what was being aired in the cab. National Public Radio was debating the cost of capital punishment versus the cost of life in prison without parole. Dr. Martin Cochran's name was mentioned and his case briefly explored, because he was the next death row inmate scheduled to be executed.

A Google search also revealed six other references to Dr. Cochran. The first was carried in the *Tacoma Times*, which recorded on Friday, May 19, 1995, that Dr. Martin Cochran, an anesthesiologist living in Tacoma, was arrested outside his former residence. It said that the doctor's estranged wife had called the cops and reported a restraining order violation. According to Mrs. Cindy Cochran, the doctor was harassing her. He'd come to his former home, beat on the door, and demanded to see his child. The doctor told the arresting officers and the magistrate that he simply knocked on the door to take his son, Marcus, for the weekend. The article went on to say that 911 received a call for help at 6:47 p.m. from Mrs. Cochran, who reported that Dr. Cochran had arrived fifteen minutes early and, therefore, was in clear violation of the restraining order. When the police arrived, Mrs. Cochran demanded that the father of her child be arrested and his visitation rights be suspended. Dr. Cochran spent the weekend in the county jail.

The next article of interest was published on August 2, 1995, in the South Carolina newspaper, the *Columbia Herald*. It detailed the murder of Thomas Thornton, a private investigator whose body had been discovered at the Greenfield Tennis Club.

Mr. Thornton had been in Columbia attending a conference on investigative techniques. He was found dangling from a large oak tree, only instead of having a rope noose around his neck, in its place was a tennis racquet, minus strings, which had been fitted over his head. He died of asphyxiation, probably because a brand new yellow tennis ball with "Tacoma Tennis Tourney" on it had been shoved into his mouth so forcefully that his two front teeth had been knocked out.

Dr. Cochran was mentioned as a "person of interest," because he was a member of the Tacoma Tennis Club and had recently employed the deceased.

The third reference to the good doctor was a wedding announcement in the *Springfield Bugle,* which reported that Miss Cindy Jenkins was to wed Dr. Martin Cochran on Saturday, June 6, 1987, at 2:30 p.m. The wedding was to take place at Westminster Presbyterian Church. Miss Jenkins had been a life-long member of the Westminster congregation, was a graduate of Springfield High, and had earned a BA in Psychology at The University of Illinois at Springfield. Dr. Cochran was a resident of Tacoma, Washington, where he practiced as an anesthesiologist. He earned his medical degree at

Stanford University, and he was a decorated war veteran, having served in Vietnam as a Force Recon Marine. The color photo of the young couple portrayed a handsome Martin, clean shaven, short haired, and ruggedly handsome. He had the strong confident look of someone who had survived adversity. He had bright eyes, a square chiseled chin, and a lady killer smile.

The soon-to-be Mrs. Cochran was absolutely stunning, one of the prettiest young women that I'd ever seen. Her oval face was framed by honey-blonde hair; her eyes shone with the delight of a young, bliss-filled lover. Smooth, clear skin, a petite nose, and full, inviting lips completed the smiling Scandinavian portrait. Additionally, the photo displayed the upper portion of Cindy's dress and it was obvious that she owned more than just a pretty face. Dr. Cochran was a lucky man indeed.

Just as I finished reading the short wedding announcement, the alarm on my Blackberry sounded. It reminded me it was time to prepare for a conference I was to attend that evening. I closed the laptop and began to sort through my suitcase. I chose a light grey pinstripe suit, a white, brushed cotton shirt, and a burgundy tie with small blue stars. As I ironed most of the wrinkles out of the shirt, I thought about the evening's lecture. The American Psychological Association was holding a symposium at the Crowne Plaza Times Square Hotel in Manhattan.

Members of the Association would be lecturing on and then discussing, "Marriage: Modern Stressors, Conflict Resolution, and Survival Skills." I had planned for this to complete the information gathering process necessary to write the column on Divorce in the Military, but a niggling thought whispered that the Cochran affair should also be included.

The conference was informative and fairly interesting, but the most fascinating part of the night was a person I met during the break. David Barnwell stood in front of me in a refreshment line and asked for a glass of Chardonnay and a black coffee. He sipped from the wine glass, turned, and bumped into me. A small amount of each beverage splashed out of its container. My eyes grew wide. It seemed as though my expensive suit was about to be soiled. I jumped back a bit and fairly yelled, "Excuse me!"

"Oh sir," came the immediate reply, "please do pardon *me!* I'm so very sorry. You *must* forgive my clumsiness!"

I did, and I said as much, accepting a cup of coffee from the attendant and starting toward the door for some fresh air. Mr. Barnwell had stepped back a few feet and was waiting to further apologize. He turned out to be a delightful older gentleman, very proper and full of Southern manners. He was from South Carolina, had been a criminal defense attorney, but was now a psychologist with a thriving practice in Charleston.

We briefly commented on a couple of the topics that had been discussed by the Association's expert panel, and it seemed as if we were like minded. He believed that people rushed into and out of marriage too quickly, and felt as though couples spent more energy seeking personal gains and revenge than they did on conflict resolution. The word "revenge" stuck in my mind

Then it occurred to me to ask him about the Dr. Cochran affair.

"The death row Dr. Cochran?" he asked, just as the end of the break was announced over the PA speaker.

"Yes. I think he's scheduled to be executed next Tuesday," I said, as we began to return to our seats. Barnwell quickly stated that he had followed, with interest, the odd tale of the murdered private investigator and his accused assassin. Before we parted, I asked him to join me for a drink and a bite to eat after the conference. I wanted to hear what he knew about the murder and Dr. Cochran.

In the hotel's lounge, "Broadway 49," we both ordered an appetizer and shared a bottle of Shiraz. Initially, we entertained a couple of interesting ideas discussed at the symposium and engaged in some small talk. After ten minutes or so, we got around to the Dr. Cochran matter.

Incredibly, a classmate of Mr. Barnwell's had been the District Attorney at the time of Dr. Cochran's murder trial, and they'd discussed the case a couple of times during and after the trial. According to Barnwell's friend, the most notable characteristic of the accused murderer was his calm demeanor. Cochran seemed always at ease—almost satisfied. It was as if he had accomplished his mission, and could now relax and relish the victory, no matter the consequences.

Although Cochran had been crafty—there were no witnesses to the hanging of the private investigator—there *was* circumstantial evidence, and it was strong. The District Attorney's case revolved around the private eye's notebook, a sales receipt for the tennis racquet found around Thornton's neck, and a receipt for two cans of Wilson extra heavy duty tennis balls stamped with the Tacoma Tennis Tournament logo—exactly like the one found crammed into the victim's mouth.

3

Back in Dallas

I returned to Dallas the next day. During the long flight, I organized the information I was to use in my column on Military Divorces, but the Cochran affair crept into my thoughts all too often. I found myself wondering how I could include it in the article.

Over the next couple of days, I shaped and fine tuned my assigned story. I had to hustle, because the piece was scheduled to appear in the following Sunday's edition, and my editor usually needed three days to approve or reject the first submission. I barely turned in the draft on time, because I couldn't keep from thinking about and checking into the Cochran story.

During a morning break on Friday, I looked into the Marine Corps Force Recon involvement in Vietnam. I learned that Force Recon Marines were deployed in small groups of between two and six men. Their mission was to sneak around—usually behind enemy lines—and collect information about enemy strength and location. Sometimes, these elite Marines carried out special operations aimed at individual targets. Their kill ratio was about four times greater than that of other Marines. Their training included learning the arts of stealth, survival, and patience. It is said that a Recon Marine can remain almost motionless for hours, and can survive without food or water for three days, patiently gathering intelligence, or awaiting the moment a target moves within elimination range. The Recons contributed significantly during Vietnam. Since you can find almost anything on the Internet, I decided to look up Recon comrades of Martin Cochran, and I got very lucky.

Dan Cannon, former Marine Corps Captain, lived in Fort Worth. He answered his phone on the second ring, at 10:15 a.m., and I introduced myself and politely asked a few questions. He held back at first, but then relaxed and retold some war stories for me. He recalled Cochran and said that he couldn't believe how things had turned out for him. He had carried out several missions with Sgt. Cochran, and noted that the sergeant had been an outstanding marine, a credit to the Corps—"the type of man that you could trust with your life." Sgt. Martin Cochran was easy going, hard working, dedicated, and dependable. He performed admirably and had even received a Purple Heart.

"A Purple Heart," I said. "So he was wounded, huh?"

"Yeah, a couple of times, in fact."

"Can you tell me about it?"

"Well," the former Captain replied, "the first time we were scouting about twenty clicks north of the DMZ near Laos. We caught Charlie patrolling near a village and shadowed them back to their camp. After dark, we sneaked in and wasted them all. Only thing was, we didn't know they had more guys out on patrol, and they came running when they heard us blasting away. One of our guys was hit and killed. Martin fell when a grenade exploded close by, and Corporal Lance and I were captured by two gooks. One bayoneted me in the arm and the other knocked out Corporal Lance with his rifle butt.

14

They tied us up and repeatedly kicked us and spat on us. I was certain that we were going to be killed.

"They tied wire around our necks, connecting us to each other. And in the morning, they forced us to march toward what we believed to be their base of operations. After about thirty minutes on the trail, I heard one of the yellow bastards say something, and the other one yanked hard on the wire, pulling us to the ground. The younger gook smacked Lance in the head again and held his rifle barrel to my mouth, while the other Commie searched the bushes. That guy never came back. Instead, Sergeant Cochran rose from behind some trees and gunned down our guard. Cochran had shrapnel in his chest and both legs. Still, he rescued us and was able to get back home on his own. I owe him my life."

"God," I said, "that's terrible. But bravo for Cochran. Can you tell me about any other times?"

"Yeah well, he was damn lucky. I wasn't in on this one. He was on patrol and got pinned down in a firefight with a squad of NVC, just he and three other marines. Two of our men got it. Martin and Torres were captured. A couple of days later, we overran the Commies' position and Cochran was rescued. Of course, they'd messed with him pretty bad. He spent a few days in a medical unit and three weeks in Nha Trang, recovering. He was never the same. Oh, he was still top-notch, performed admirably, but he didn't talk much. When he did, it was mostly about revenge. I think he was discharged about five months later."

I envisioned all sorts of torture Cochran might have suffered and wondered how the trauma had affected his life. I asked Cannon if he was aware of Tuesday's scheduled execution. He said, "No," that he hadn't heard anything about Martin in years. He said that if I wrote a story about Cochran I should include all the heroic, selfless acts he'd performed in 'Nam.

"We were all trained to be killers," he said, "but it's hard for me to believe that Martin would've used his skills in a non-combat situation. I guess the divorce really got to him. He flipped, Mr. Fontaine. He must've gone insane—Martin Cochran the murderer was not the same guy who saved my life. I wish I could talk to him now, remind him of who he was and thank him once again."

Cannon paused a few moments, then said, "I wonder if I could get a call or letter through to him before Tuesday?"

A great question, I thought, and I wondered how I could get in touch with the condemned man, interview him, and maybe pass along Cannon's message.

We ended our conversation, and I hung up the phone and sat for a while studying the situation. How had an exemplary military man, a hero, a healer become a murderer? What had happened during the divorce? Why would he have killed a private eye and tortured his ex-love? Had the former iron-willed Marine surrendered to hatred and revenge? Now, I was really hooked. Could I interview the doctor before Tuesday?

By lunchtime on Friday, I had completed the column on military divorce. I ended it with a teaser, mentioning Cochran's impending execution, his just reward for misbehavior following a divorce, and a line that indicated I'd follow up on his saga. I emailed a copy of the draft to my editor and planned to present a paper copy to him that afternoon.

As Kelly and I ate grilled cheese sandwiches and chips, I told her about the Cochran case, which I hadn't mentioned until then. She was surprised that I hadn't, since it was obvious I was engrossed with the story.

Clearly irritated she asked, "Why is our society so interested in murder and horrible crimes committed against innocent people? Why should we care about someone who's taken loved ones away from families, or who've left people to endure tortured memories for the rest of their lives?"

We searched each other's eyes. Then she continued, "Why are there so many more stories about people in gangs and prison than there are stories about the victims of crime?"

I told her I didn't know, but it was true more people would rather watch a show about gangland murders than a show about happy, well-adjusted families living in suburbia. I knew she was really asking me why I cared about Cochran, and just not directly confronting me.

I left for the office with the draft in my briefcase and an uneasy feeling in my stomach. As I drove, I rehearsed what I would say to my editor about the military divorce piece, and I thought of an angle to present to him so I could write a follow-up article on Cochran.

When I arrived at the office, the boss was busy. His door was closed, and the secretary gave me the look that said, "Don't mess with him right now, and when you do go in, be careful!"

I went to my cubicle, checked my in-box, and answered a few emails. When all of the scut work was done and it looked like I had some time to kill, I Googled Cindy Jenkins and then Mrs. Cindy Cochran. Of course, there were zillions of hits for Cindy Jenkins and Cindy Cochran. I narrowed the search results by typing "divorce of Martin and Cindy Cochran/Tacoma."

There wasn't much about the divorce, but I found the article covering the doctor's restraining order violation *and* an announcement stating that the divorce had been recorded by the Clerk of Courts in Tacoma. I reread the wedding announcement and kept on searching. Then, I hit pay dirt.

On December 14, 1995, in Albany, NY, a woman was found in a white Chevy van. It had been parked near the loading dock of St. Peter's Hospital for two days, before a security guard heard noises coming from inside it and investigated.

When the van was opened, the guards discovered a woman securely tied to an old Army cot. Two-inch, cloth medical tape was wrapped around her arms and legs, binding her to the wooden side supports of the cot. Her face was covered by surgical bandages, and she was shaking the cot violently and screaming as loud as possible through the bandages. Cindy Jenkins was hysterical, dehydrated, and severely mutilated.

Mutilated? My imagination ran wild. I knew what the word meant, but consulted the dictionary anyway: *". . . to cause severe damage to [a body . . .], to ruin the beauty of something, to severely damage or spoil something."*

Mutilated. The idea seemed much more sinister than murder; a purposeful insanity bent on ruin rather than eradication; premeditated evil deeds meant to have horrific lasting effects; actions enjoyed while being executed; results to be admired by the fiend; revenge on display; punishment for all to see.

Cochran must be a madman.

The hospital spokesman didn't go into fine details, but did say Ms. Jenkins was thought to be near death. Police suspected her ex-husband had kidnapped her, tortured her, and left her alive to suffer a lifetime of humiliating disfigurement. But it *wasn't* attempted murder.

I read the news article twice, then sat staring at the computer screen for several minutes, envisioning the macabre scene. The phone rang. The boss was ready to see me.

It took a few moments for me to erase the nightmarish image the article had conjured up in my mind. Slowly, I collected my report and headed to Harry's office. He was obviously perturbed. He'd just finished a conference call with the big wigs, who were not happy about decreased revenue, increased costs, and the impending sale of the company. He shared some of the conversation with me and expressed his concerns.

After he settled down a bit, we got around to my piece. He'd skimmed through it earlier, and basically liked it, but, of course, needed a little more time with it. I gave him the paper copy and thanked him for his initial approval. Then, I suggested that I thought I had a great story in the making, summarized what I knew of the Cochran tale, and added that it could be tied to the military divorce column, *or* it could stand on its own as an example of divorces gone horribly wrong.

Harry listened, but squirmed as I spoke. He already had a new assignment for me. I was to report on how the current drought in Texas had affected some big businesses, and how the lack of rain water affects big cattle ranches, oil operations, chemical plants, and such in the Dallas/Ft. Worth area.

"You're shittin' me," I said. "Do you really think people would rather read about the troubles a drought causes millionaire cattlemen or Exxon than a juicy story about infidelity, revenge, torture and murder?"

Harry didn't blink. "I need you to report on the drought's effect on big business around here. Okay, Pierre?"

4

Prison Bound

I returned home disappointed. Cochran made a better story than a drought. Nobody cared if Exxon's multi-billion dollar profits were reduced to only a few billion because Mother Nature wouldn't rain—*everybody* cared that a heinous villain got his just reward for murdering and maiming innocent people. Kelly even agreed, after she read the article about the ex-Mrs. Cochran being found in the van.

I moped around the house. After supper I began to look into the current drought statistics and pulled up recent news reports of big businesses around Dallas, but my heart wasn't into it—and I was too irritable. My thoughts kept returning to the description of Cindy bound to the cot and screaming through bloody bandages.

Countless questions raced through my mind: What kind of madman had Martin Cochran become? What had happened during the divorce? What kind of hell had Cindy lived through? What was her story now? What would the condemned doctor have to say now? Would he have gotten religion in prison like so many other criminals did? Would he now be sorry for his monstrous crimes?

I couldn't pay attention to my new assignment *until* I had answers to some of my questions. I had a few days before Cochran's execution. Perhaps I could visit him somehow. But would he agree to an interview?

Checking into South Carolina's death row visitation policies, I discovered that only people who are on a prisoner's visitation list are allowed to visit. My mind raced to figure out a way to contact him, get my name on his list, and interview him. Maybe David Barnwell could guide me to the most expedient method. I called him. He was surprised, but happy to hear from me.

Barnwell said that our conversation had sparked in him a renewed interest in the Cochran case. He had, just the day before, phoned his old buddy and former District Attorney, Quinton McMillan, to get an update on Cochran. McMillan hadn't offered anything new, but said that he did know the warden, and that he might see him at a fund raiser that Saturday evening.

"What luck!" I said. "Do you think I could contact Mr. McMillan? Do you think he might help me get on Cochran's visitor list?"

Barnwell chuckled and gave me his classmate's phone number.

Quinton McMillan, Attorney at Law, was not thrilled to hear from me, but suffered through my introduction and reason for contacting him. He said that, of course, he was familiar with the war hero turned maniac, but he had no more information on Cochran other than Tuesday's execution date. I explained that I'd like to interview Dr. Cochran if possible, but I needed to contact him and be placed on his visitors list. McMillan cleared his throat loudly and was silent for a long moment. He said that *he* couldn't help me, but if I were to attend the Dorchester County Battered Women's Shelter fund raiser tomorrow night, I might be able to petition the warden in person.

"Do you think he'd help?" I asked.

McMillan didn't answer. Instead, he hung up the phone. I cursed the pompous old bastard, got online, and purchased an airplane ticket to Charleston, South Carolina.

While I packed a suitcase, Kelly chewed me out. I had no business going to South Carolina, or poking my nose into Martin Cochran's crazy story, she said. I'd been given an assignment and should pay attention to that. Plus, we were almost broke. We didn't have enough money to go chasing after some lunatic a thousand miles away.

She was right, but my reporter's curiosity was in overdrive. I said I'd dip into our overdraft account, and promised that I would work late that night, and every available minute during the trip, on the drought story. I just had to try my hardest to interview Cochran before his death in four days.

I don't like fund raisers, but I put on a smile at the event, and showed respectful concern for the cause. I mingled with the invited guests, and, on trips around the dinning hall, I tried to spy where the warden would be seated; two hundred dollars had bought me a seat within sight of his appointed table.

At six thirty, the first of three speakers took the podium and everyone got seated. The warden wore a dark blue, wool suit, and spit-shined, black leather shoes. He sported a crew cut, pencil-thin mustache, and a deep tan. His eyes were penetratingly sharp, and he *looked* like a warden: stern, stiff, by the book. His demeanor screamed, "Don't even think about talking to me or asking me a favor."

I did anyway.

Warden W. T. Moretz was nicer than he appeared. He kindly listened to my request and then said, "Boy, you've got a lot a nerve to come all this way and pay two hundred dollars just to ask me a question. But I don't think I can help you. First of all, it's not my job or place to arrange visitors for anybody. Secondly, Cochran doesn't have a visitor list. He never sees anyone—hasn't had a visitor since I've known him. *Newsweek* tried to interview him about seven years ago, but he wouldn't talk. He's very quiet, does calisthenics, and writes in his journal. I hear he'll talk to the guards some and to the chaplain. There's absolutely no way he's gonna entertain a reporter during his last days on earth." He laughed and whispered something to the woman seated to his right. She laughed too.

"Finally, Mr. Fontaine," he added, "I can't help you because Cochran was transferred two weeks ago. He's now incarcerated at Broad River, where the death chamber is located, and I'm not the warden there."

My heart sank. Kelly had been right—I shouldn't have come here. I should have been in Dallas writing a boring column on the Texas drought. I should drop my fascination with Cochran. I stood spellbound, searching the warden's face for any sign of backing down from his refusal to help. But he stared back at me like the Sphinx. During those few moments, my mind whirred. Did I have a final card to play? Was there any more to say other than thank you?

As he extended his hand to shake mine and dismiss me, a thought burst through the fog: "Well, if there is any way, sir, could you let him know that his old Marine

24

buddy, Captain Cannon, sends his prayers and a final thank you for saving his life in 'Nam?"

Warden Moretz gripped my hand a little tighter and knitted his brow. A quizzical expression replaced the "see ya' later buster" look.

"I'd forgotten he was in Vietnam. Decorated, right?"

"Yes, sir, Purple Heart."

"Hmmm . . . I was in the Corps. Twenty-one-and-a-half years. Two tours in 'Nam."

He thought for a second, then said quietly, "I'll see what I can do. Semper Fi."

He released my hand, and, when he did, I gave him my card. On the back I quickly wrote: MY PRAYERS. GOD SPEED. THANKS AGAIN. CPT. CANNON.

I thanked Warden Moretz and made a beeline for the parking lot.

Broad River Correctional Institute is located in Columbia. I was eighty-eight miles away from the "Death House." Who knew that Death Row and the Death Chamber were not side-by-side in the same facility? I bet that arrogant old fart McMillan did and he had sent me to the wrong place on purpose.

It was a long night in the hotel room, but I did get some work done on my real assignment. At eleven o'clock, I took a break and watched the local news. Near the end of the broadcast, the co-anchor spent about two minutes reminding the audience that, "Convicted murderer, Dr. Martin Cochran will be put to death by lethal injection at six p.m. on Tuesday. Cochran was found guilty of murdering private investigator Thomas Thornton in August of 1995. The death sentence will be carried out at the Broad River Capitol Punishment Facility at Central Correctional Institute in Columbia. Cochran's attorneys have promised no last minute maneuvers to delay the punishment. Civil Rights groups and anti-capital punishment organizations from around the country have vowed to protest. Cochran will be the first convicted killer to be put to death in South Carolina in more than two years, and the seventh death row inmate executed in the U.S. this year."

Several times through the night I awoke with hopeless feelings. It seemed unlikely I'd ever interview Cochran. I pictured Kelly wagging her finger at me saying, "I told ya so," and giving me hell for buying the spur-of-the-moment, super-expensive plane ticket that further drained our anemic bank account.

After awakening from a dream in which Kelly and I had a huge argument, I promised to board a plane at daybreak, return to Dallas and surrender any interest in Dr. Martin Cochran. But when daylight finally arrived, I made up my mind to stay in Columbia. I would petition the Broad River warden for permission to speak with Cochran, and, at the very least, attempt to interview witnesses to the execution. Hopefully, the family of Thomas Thornton and maybe even the ex-Mrs. Cochran would be there and want to talk. Now wouldn't that be something. Surely, the madman's surviving victim would come to watch Satan pay for his sins.

The morning newscast reported the same stories as were covered the previous night, including Tuesday's scheduled execution. I watched it again. What was our fascination with death really about? I asked myself. I explored the subject for a few minutes and then turned my attention to the drought story. Sometime around

8:30 a.m., I left a message on the voice mail of Frieda Sheehan, the secretary of the Communications Department at Central Correctional Institute, stating my name and reason for calling. I was requesting to speak with the warden regarding Dr. Cochran, and I left my cell phone number. I had forgotten that since it was Sunday the office staff and warden might have the day off.

By two fifteen, I had left two more messages. When I didn't hear back, I gave up on hearing from them until Monday. Again, I felt like a fool.

For most of the rest of the day, I worked on the drought story. But, during an afternoon break, I took a stroll around the city. Columbia is a bustling Southern city of about 100,000 folks, and, on this beautiful June Sunday, almost all of them were out and about. I walked downtown and poked around the shops. The city had recently gone through an aggressive revitalization. The city parks were clean, green, and shaded by beautiful deciduous trees: oak, maple, sycamore, and others that I didn't recognize. There was a thriving Arts District and the wonderful Three Rivers Greenway. It was odd to think of all this life and vitality while only a couple of miles away, under the same gorgeous sky, sat the death chamber and Dr. Cochran.

Monday morning was a repeat of Sunday. I *had* to leave a message. By nine thirty, Frieda had not called back, so I phoned her again. She said that she would relay the message when the warden came in. I called two more times by two o'clock, and the secretary was obviously tired of me. I was losing all hope. Apparently, returning a journalist's call is not a high priority of prison officials.

At a quarter to four, I gave up on anyone calling me, and drove to the prison. I showed my Texas driver's license and *Dallas Daily* photo ID to the guard, and stated my business. He called the warden's office, spoke briefly to someone, and turned back to me.

"You do not have an appointment, Mr. Fontaine, and Warden Phillips doesn't have time to see you today," he stated with a smirk and a twinkle in his eye. "I'm sorry, but you'll have to make an appointment and come back some other time."

My heart sank. I was defeated. I turned and walked slowly to the car, pointed the vehicle at the highway, and hit the gas a bit too hard. I came to a halt at the stop sign, prepared to pack it in and give up on this whole crazy mess, when my cell phone rang.

"Mr. Fontaine?" an unfamiliar voice asked.

"Yes."

"This is Carlton Willcox, Chaplain at Broad River. I hope that I'm not interfering with any of your plans. I understand that you had a conversation with Warden Moretz. I was at the dinner Saturday evening, and he passed along the message from Captain Cannon to Dr. Cochran. I gave your card to Martin and he wishes to visit with you if you have time."

I was speechless. I was so surprised that I turned off the engine to hear whatever else the chaplain might have to say. A shrieking horn blast from behind jarred me back to reality. I nearly dropped the phone as I restarted the car and blurted out, "Yes, yes, yes sir! I did speak to the warden and I'd love to visit with Dr. Cochran!" I cut a U-turn and zoomed back into the parking lot.

We continued our conversation, as I parked within sight of the guard house. The guard listened to the chaplain via my cell phone, but must not have believed his ears. He had that "sure buddy" look of disbelief, as the conversation began. He insisted that the chaplain call on the guard house phone, and enter my name on the visitation list.

I sat on a freshly painted prison park bench while the guard ate crow. Soon the guard's phone rang. He spoke briefly and accessed the computer.

"Mr. Fontaine," he spat, "visitation hours begin at six p.m. Come back then. It'll take about fifteen minutes to process you and escort you in."

I'd been in county jails before, interviewing cons for various reasons, even been in a women's prison once. So, I was mentally prepared for the pat down search and the metal detector wand, but I wasn't prepared for the feelings I got while walking through maximum-security prison hallways to the visitation room in the death house.

Immediately behind the guard shack there were two rows of cyclone fence topped with coils of razor wire, and a fence-enclosed tunnel that led from the front gate to the indestructible metal portal of the maximum-security fortress. Guards and iron doors and buzzers and razor wire and snipers on high—my head began to swim, and my heart pounded. The polished tile floors and deafening prison acoustics assaulted my senses. Claustrophobia smothered me. It was hard to breathe. The clicking of each footstep was like an electric shock to my eardrums. The ceilings were dangerously low and the hallways too narrow—they threatened to crush me. Sweat rolled down my forehead. I envisioned marching past dozens of depraved maniacs, who would grab for me through cell bars, who would solicit me for sexual favors, or promise torturous treatment if they could only reach me. I knew that they'd watch my ass, fantasize about its virginity, and spit on me before I got out of range.

Get a grip, Pierre.

Thankfully, I arrived at the Visitation Room unharmed. I'd been terrified, but it was all in my head. The room was well lit and obviously secure. No one could possibly break through the thick Plexiglas separating prisoners and guests. The guard escorted me to booth "C" and I waited. Soon, a man approached the other side of the booth and sat. He picked up the battered, black plastic telephone receiver. My heart thumped. I was now face to face with Dr. Martin Cochran, convicted killer and torturer—a madman. I gripped the telephone receiver and placed it to my ear.

"Mr. Fontaine, I presume," said Cochran.

"Dr. Cochran," I replied. He still resembled the man in the wedding announcement photo. His hair was longer, and he was pale with facial creases that spoke of age. He didn't have any visible prison tattoos, but his eyes reflected the years of solitude-induced lunacy. At first, he didn't look directly at me, but when he did it was as if lasers bored through my pupils and tore into my soul.

He smirked as he said, "You may call me Martin. What took you so long, Pierre?"

He paused for an extended moment while his laser vision ripped through my face and left an indelible mark on my psyche. "I figured that you'd have come last year or last month," he said, at last.   He finally blinked, took a deep breath and held it while awaiting my reply.

I was confused.   What did he mean?   I had only learned of him this week.

"It's too late now," he continued.   "There's not enough time. I die tomorrow," he calmly remarked.

I asked what he was talking about and said that I'd only found out about him five days ago.

"You've come to watch me die, to witness my final breath, to insure that I've paid the price. Has Cindy sent you? Have you come to write a book about me? Then make it into a movie and get rich."

I was flabbergasted.   I honestly hadn't even considered such a thing, and told him so.   But, in that very instant I knew he was right.   I was too intrigued by what little I already knew. I couldn't simply talk to him and walk away. A follow-up story to the military divorce article was not enough.   I must uncover the whole story and tell the rest of the world.

"How is the Captain?" Martin asked, almost in a whisper.

5

Conversation with a Madman

I said that Captain Cannon was doing well and he sent Cochran his sincere best wishes. I recounted our phone conversation and asked if the doctor would like the captain's number. I repeated what Cannon had said, "I'd like to thank him once again for saving my life in 'Nam."

A different kind of expression shone on the criminal's face when I mentioned the war. It was as if he was reviewing video footage of missions and firefights. His laser stare softened and his jaw muscles relaxed. He seemed to focus his gaze on some point above my head.

"Have you ever killed anyone, Pierre?"

"What?" I shook my head. "No." *What an insane question. What kind of crazy have I got here?*

He continued to inspect the ceiling above me.

"Aaah, the first time ya freak out a little bit, but then after a while, you settle down and learn to enjoy the hunt and the victory."

My eyes widened. I couldn't believe what I was hearing. Was he going to confess to murder?

"The most thrilling moment is when the enemy realizes that he's going to die. Now, you haven't slammed the blade home yet, or pulled the trigger—but they know that you're about to end their life. Their eyes get very big. They take great gulps of air. They may whimper or moan, or even beg for mercy. But it's of no use. Their fate has been sealed. Really, the end is a relief for them. No more anticipation. No more worry of torture or pain. Their last breaths are like the fireworks on Independence Day! I love killing."

His laser vision returned and burned a hole in my face.

"What do *you* love, Pierre?"

I nearly crapped in my pants. *Is this guy for real?* My breath caught, and I squirmed in my chair. This nutcase actually enjoys killing and isn't afraid to flaunt it. He really *is* insane.

"Did the Captain tell ya about Duc Tho, or the time I was captured?" He leaned forward, bringing his face as close to the partition as possible.

"He said you'd been captured once, but got away. He mostly talked about you saving him and Lance, and a couple of his missions around Saigon before the fall."

"Captured . . . yes, imprisoned and not unlike here," replied Cochran. "Maybe we'll talk about that later. In Duc Tho, we musta spent the best part of three days waiting on some NVC Colonel. We were half submerged in a rice paddy with nothin' to eat. We sipped the putrid, stinking water and pissed in our pants, holding perfectly still waiting—just waiting. The yellow bastard never showed. We were starved and pruned as shit before the captain decided to move out. On the way back home, we ran across a little village, and decided to nab something to eat. About midnight I garroted the teenage guard, and we moved in.

"We finished a couple of gooks silently with our Ka-Bars and scored their mess. Charlie's cold rice wasn't good, but it kept us from starving. Anyway, we found a couple of our boys in the latrine, staked down in the shit —naked, with bamboo spikes driven through their family jewels, their arms, and legs. Both were near death from infection and beatings. Private Roos was still alert enough to beg us to kill him. He knew he wasn't going to survive. He begged and cried and pleaded. He ordered the captain to shoot him in the head. Neither of us could do it, even though we both knew he was right. He was definitely going to die. After about an hour, Cannon handed Roos his .45, put it in his right hand with the barrel pointing towards the private's head. Roos thanked the Captain, closed his eyes, took a deep breath, and blew out his own brains. His eyes popped open as his head exploded. I'll never forget that look: resolve, surprise, release, death, peace." Cochran smiled as his voice faded.

My God! This is insane. Why is he telling me this? I felt like I was talking to Hannibal Lecter. We were both silent for a minute. He studied me, a leer on his face. He searched my eyes and then aimed his lasers at what he could see of my torso. Finally, he examined my hands. I twisted. What did he see? Was he simply looking for my reaction? Playing me for a fool? Or was he considering, if he had the chance, the most entertaining method of killing me?

I cursed myself. *This guy is too nuts. This idea is nuts. How can I interview him?* How could his story ever be my professional salvation? Why would anybody care about Martin Cochran?

"Do you really want me to interview you, Dr. Cochran?" I asked hesitantly. "Do you honestly think that I came to see you die and write a book about you?"

He cracked a little smile and nodded his head up and down.

"Well then, I guess that I'll ask a few questions."

The smile turned into a smirk.

"Okay, Martin, what happened to you? How did you to go from a decorated war hero to a death row inmate? Just how did this all begin?"

He tilted his chin upward and stared through the ceiling. After considering his response, he resumed burning holes through my face, and stated, "In the beginning, God created the Heavens and the Earth. The Earth was without form and all was dark . . ."

What the hell? What kind of crazy answer is that ? What have I gotten myself into? I'm in the middle of a maximum security prison visiting a convicted lunatic who'll be executed tomorrow. I've got about ninety minutes to interview him, and he's rambling on about Genesis *and looking at me like I'm his next victim.*

I maintained my silence and anticipatory expression while he closed his eyes, bowed his head slightly and took in a deep breath. "In the beginning," he softly spoke into the telephone receiver, "I was a small boy, growing up in a small town, the son of a small man and a small woman. I was clay. And they molded me. I went to school like all the other children, and I played ball, hide and seek, and other games just like all the kids. I was like the Garden of Eden, beautiful, pure." He paused. "I was like the Earth before the light, full of promise." He returned his gaze to me and sat still.

I watched him for a second. I was bewildered. I rearranged my butt, then asked, "Martin, what does all that mean? Where'd you grow up? What was your childhood like? Your family?"

He rallied his sanity and answered that he was born to a hardworking couple in Cincinnati. His father was an auto mechanic, who slaved day and night to provide for his family. He was always greasy, dirty, and tired.

He pushed Martin hard to become a professional, to get an education and a good job. Martin's mom was a devoted wife and mother. She made money by mending neighbors' clothes. She held Martin to very high standards. She shackled him with chores meant to prepare him for life's challenges, and insisted he attend church each Sunday. Childhood had been happy enough. He learned to work hard. He did well in school, and even had a semester of college before he was drafted.

Instead of being forced into the Army, he chose to join the Marine Corps. The Corps was where he belonged, according to "Sarge," a neighbor, who had retired from the Marines. Martin excelled in the military. He obeyed his superiors, worked hard, and was promoted quickly. He found his niche as a Force Recon. He loved the training. He loved being stealthy, gathering information, and being part of small elite teams with more independence than regular Marines.

"Now," Cochran said, "that's how I started. How did *you* start off, Pierre? Who are *you*? I want to know what kind of person is going to write my book."

I recounted my youth, summarized it in a nutshell. We had similar stories, though *I* did not join the military.

When I finished detailing my college days, he shook his head and said, "That's a terribly boring story, Pierre, but I'll bet that you are now a successful man. Am I correct?"

I nodded.

He went on, "I thought so. And I'll bet you've worked hard to become successful."

I nodded again.

"Now, how would you feel if all that you'd worked for was taken away? What if suddenly you had nothing—no wife, no house, no job. What if the person you trusted the most lied to you—cheated? What if she stole away with your child and got him killed? What if your reputation was ruined, all of your schooling wasted? Would you become angry? Depressed? Would you lash out at whoever was behind the scheme that ruined you? What would you do? Would you seek revenge? Would you fight back, Pierre, or roll over, take it in the ass, and wish the bitch well?"

"I don't know. I've never really thought about it," I answered.

"Well think about it now. What would you do? Suddenly you have nothing, and the woman of your dreams is screwing another man. Would ya take it? Would ya kill 'em, or happily sign the papers and skip off into the sunset?"

"Well, I'd be angry, I'm sure."

"So, Pierre, you've never been divorced, lost it all?"

"No."

"Well how in hell are you going to write a book about me if you've never felt the pain of love lost, of betrayal, of infidelity?" Then, louder, "How can you write about something that you've never experienced? Are you planning on saying that I just went nuts? That I started killing and cutting for no good reason!? She *deserved* it! She stole my life and so, I stole hers. An eye for an eye. An eye for an eye!" he shouted.

He had suddenly stood up, and he charged the Plexiglas, the receiver held to his left ear, with his right index finger pointing at me like the trigger of a cocked pistol. His laser eyes burned white hot, and spittle arched towards me as he verbally gored me. The sudden motion caused me to jump back, and I overturned my wooden chair and dropped the telephone. I nearly sprawled on the floor. The noise from all of the commotion brought the guards into both sides of the visitation suite. The one on my side shook his head at me as though I were a bumbling fool. Cochran's guard took the doctor by the shoulder, said something, and signaled me to hang up the receiver.

The visit was over.

I couldn't believe it. Over?

That's *all*? There wasn't going to be a book written with this little information—not even a column for the paper. What a waste of time. I really felt foolish.

As I slinked past the guard, he tapped me on the shoulder and pointed in the direction of booth "C." I turned and saw Martin reseated, holding the telephone out toward me, and wearing an apologetic expression. He motioned for me to return. And I did. He meekly said that he was sorry for the outburst. Lunacy at bay again. He said that we only had twenty minutes left to visit and that he would explain why he became angry enough to kill. He spoke rapidly and to the point, no more parables. His face changed, the lasers cooled, the madness faded. I could see the scars on his soul left by a failed marriage, a lovers' scorn, a life lost to anger and revenge.

Cindy had been a beautiful prize, his crowning achievement, the love of his life. When they met, she was young, vibrant, mysterious, enchanting—a true treasure. She completed him. He adored her and showered her with attention and gifts. Their early years were bliss. Of course, there were difficulties. His career demanded that he spend many hours away from her, at the hospital, at the clinic and at meetings. But at first, she didn't mind so much. She would always greet him with a warm hug and kiss when he came home—no matter the hour. And she always had something tasty for him to eat. The sex was passionate, energetic, and adventurous. No complaints there.

When Cindy became pregnant, he threw a small party for her. All of her girlfriends and a couple of his buddies attended. It was a joyous occasion that seemed to weld an unbreakable bond around the new family. When Marcus was born, he was idolized. But, in the moment of his birth, something in the marriage died. Martin was no longer Cindy's top concern. Now, he would have to share time and affection with his son. Cindy poured all of her energy into nurturing young Marcus, and Martin received the leftovers.

Soon after the birth, Cindy became depressed. Her youthful liveliness waned, and interest in everything other than Marcus suffered greatly. Unfortunately, at the same time, Martin made partner in his group. The position demanded increased duties and more time spent away from his family. To combat depression, Cindy sought counseling, and began an exercise program. Her exercise plan included tennis lessons. She was already fair at the game, but, with some private coaching, she became much better.

Trip Johnson, a tennis pro at the Tacoma Tennis Club, was handsome, young, energetic, and a smooth "hands on" instructor. He became Cindy's champion—understanding supportive, encouraging. They spent many hours perfecting Cindy's serves and returns. And while Marcus was napping in the club's daycare center, the two would sometimes have lunch together. It wasn't long until they were sharing more than sandwiches and a Bloody Mary. Martin's long hours afforded many opportunities for tennis matches, tennis lessons, and shopping excursions in Trip's Chevy van. While Martin was ruggedly handsome and in good shape, he was twelve years older than Cindy, and very busy with his career. Trip, on the other hand, was two years younger than Cindy. He had the face of a movie star and the body of an Olympic athlete. His eyes were warm, soft, and inviting. His touch made Cindy melt. He paid as much attention to Cindy as she desired. They became lovers. Cindy "took lessons" almost every day — sometimes even on Martin's days off from work.

Cindy's sexual appetite for Martin waned, and he noticed. He became suspicious of all of the lessons and time spent with Trip.

"Finally, I hired a private eye to check up on my little 'Bird of Paradise,' " Martin said with a sneer, his laser eyes returning. "Thornton followed her for about three months and caught her fucking the tennis boy almost every day. While I was bustin' my ass, and Marcus was tucked away in day care, the bastard was banging my pussy and spending my money on expensive lunches and tennis crap."

I listened attentively and watched his eyes grow wilder as he became angrier and more animated.

"Do you wonder, Pierre, why I'll die tomorrow for killing Thomas Thornton, Private Investigator, instead of the cheating bitch or boy toy Tripster?"

I nodded and said, "Yes."

"Because, Pierre, I discovered — "

The phone went dead. He continued speaking, but I couldn't hear a thing. Time was up. A couple of minutes before, the guard had signaled by raising two fingers. Now, we were done. I'm sure my mouth dropped open wide. I couldn't believe it. Just like some daytime drama series, I was left hanging while the commercials played. Only this time, the ending would never be known. My heart sank again. And again I felt foolish for having begun such an impossible task. What was I thinking? One visitation wasn't long enough for Martin to tell his story. I waved good-bye to him and mouthed "good luck." The guard ushered him out of the suite. As he shuffled out, my head felt drained of blood, and my heart beat wildly as though I were the one heading to the death chamber. I returned to my hotel room depressed, a fool.

6

Confession

I phoned home and told Kelly about my day. She listened patiently. When I finished, she scolded me for wasting my time and our money. She ordered me to return home and get to work on my real assignment. We ended the conversation angry at each other. I tried to work on the drought column, but I couldn't focus. My thoughts kept returning to Martin Cochran, his scheduled death, and my unfinished interview. I reviewed what I had learned and entered all that I could recall into a file dubbed Martin's Story. I didn't know exactly what I would do with it yet, but I was determined to, at the very least, see the journey through to its end — his execution tomorrow at 6:00 p.m.

I put away my laptop about ten and tried to watch some TV, but my mind was too restless. I needed to come up with a way to write about Martin, even though our conversation had been interrupted. Maybe that was the angle: don't wait until the last minute, there is no guarantee that you'll have enough time for whatever — no, that wasn't good. It was a worn out cliché. Anyway, it was a long night filled with twisting and rolling and racing thoughts. I awoke in sweat-soaked sheets, exhausted and frustrated.

I showered and immediately set to work on the drought story before Martin or Cindy could capture my mind. At noon, Channel 10 retold some of Martin's story. It had live video footage of protest groups setting up outside the prison, and even an interview with the warden.

"This evening's execution allows loved ones to have some closure in a matter where an innocent man was prematurely taken from them. It is the result of a fair trial and the hard decisions of honest citizens," he said. "It is the end of the road for a convicted criminal who blatantly disregarded the laws of God and man. It is when Justice will finally be served."

A protester spoke next. Though sympathetic to the victim's family, she enumerated the reasons why the State should not be in the business of killing people. She was passionate and articulate. I understood both sides, and turned off the TV with a strange feeling in my gut. I promised myself to be at the prison by 4:00 p.m. Then, I got back to work.

When my cell phone rang, I was struggling with how to make Exxon Mobil's meager profit of twenty-six billion dollars, the poorest return in twelve years, seem like a crisis. The caller was Carlton Willcox, the Broad River Facility's chaplain. He greeted me and asked if I would be interested in visiting with Martin again?

"Yes, of course!" I answered.

He explained that Martin's final visitation hours would be from 2:00 to 4:00 p.m., and that the doctor had specifically requested that I arrive promptly at two.

I was there at the requested hour.

As animated as Cochran was the previous day when we parted, he was equally subdued now. His face was relaxed. He seemed resigned, at peace, as if he were already there calmly awaiting the pentothal to put him to sleep, the pancuronium to paralyze him, and the potassium chloride to stop his heart. He greeted me as warmly as one can through a half inch of bulletproof glass while speaking through a telephone.

"Thanks for coming, Pierre. I hoped that you would. I wanted to continue our conversation. Where did we leave off?"

I told him that he was about to tell me he had discovered something. I guessed it was the reason why he killed the private eye instead of Trip.

"Oh yes," Martin replied. "I was about to tell you something I never told the lawyers or the jury. I was about to confess to murder and explain how poor Mr. Thornton wound up in that tree."

I sat tight and listened.

"You see, Pierre, Mr. Thornton was supposed to only follow my wife and report on her tryst with young Trip. But he got greedy. He liked what he saw and decided to get in on the action. I found out, and somehow he had an accident in South Carolina. Unfortunately for me, the evidence suggested that someone with access to my tennis racquet had a part in his untimely demise."

Cochran rolled his eyes and grinned an evil, satisfied smile. "Poor bastard probably suffered a great deal before he died." He sat back in his wooden chair and examined the ceiling above my head just as he had yesterday.

"Pierre, did you know that in three and a half hours I will be killed by some of the same drugs that I used every day in the hospital?"

"I hadn't thought about it really," I replied.

"Yes, Mr. Fontaine, you see I think it's quite ironic that the chemicals I used to ease suffering, that put bread on my table and paid for my beautiful wife's tennis lessons are going to end my life. Do you know the procedure?"

"No—not really. I've seen a documentary or two that has re-enacted an execution, but not recently."

"Aaah, well, it's pretty interesting. Two days ago, an execution team was chosen by the warden and they have practiced the protocol several times by now. They actually count the steps from my cell to the death chamber, and time the journey. The lethal injection will occur at precisely six PM and they must know exactly when to collect me and how fast I must walk to my doom. Two IVs will be started, one in each arm. Intravenous solutions will drip into my bloodstream. If one IV doesn't work for any reason—the second will be immediately available. I'm definitely going to die a few minutes after six.

"They have practiced strapping someone to the gurney, wheeling them into the death chamber, connecting the monitors, and opening the curtain for the spectators. The warden has practiced asking if the condemned has any last words, has paused for a response, and then exited the chamber. The death squad will then press their little buttons, and the drugs will begin to flow: first the sodium pentothal, then the pancuronium, and finally, the potassium. My final trip! I'll be put to sleep, then my diaphragm will be paralyzed, then my heart will stop. I'll go limp, then stop breathing, turn blue, and meet Jesus. Wow, what a way to go, huh?!"

I couldn't believe it. This guy was *really* nuts!

"Martin how can you be so objective, so calm about this. I mean, they are going to kill you today. I don't understand how you're not freaking out," I told him, my eyes searching his for any sign of fear. But there wasn't any.

"Though I walk through the valley of the shadow of death, I will fear no evil," he replied, with his eyes closed at first, then his lasers returning to brand my face with the words "I will fear no evil."

Uh oh, that prison religion. Here we go again, I thought.

"Pierre, I've been in a cage for a dozen years, the last ten on death row. I would rather be dead than to live like this for another ten. There are many things worse than death, Mr. Fontaine."

"I believe you, Martin," I said and paused. "Hey, can I change the subject a little bit? I hate to say it, but you need to tell me everything that you can as quickly as possible, because there's not much time left."

"Really, Pierre?" he said as sarcastically as possible.

Doctor Cochran then told me about the day that he caught Thornton and Cindy screwing. Martin had not told Cindy that he had the day off from work. He left the house just as usual. At nine forty, he was stationed across the street from the Tennis Club, expecting to watch Cindy enter the club for lessons with Trip, and then leave with him an hour later. At nine fifty, she arrived with Marcus in tow. At ten fifty-three, Thornton pulled up half a block away as was his practice when spying. He walked across the street and sat on a park bench with a newspaper as a cover. In a bit, Cindy exited the club, freshly showered, and wearing large dark sunglasses, a peasant dress, and sandals. Martin expected to see Trip follow, but he didn't. Instead, he watched Cindy walk to Thornton's car. She opened the passenger door and jumped in. One minute later, Thornton got into the car and started the engine. Martin could not believe his eyes. What the hell was going on? Was Cindy screwing Thornton, too? He followed the black Cadillac and watched it pull into a sleazy motel, six blocks from the club. Cindy and Thornton exited the car separately—about a minute apart—and each hurriedly entered the building. About fifty minutes later they reversed their steps, and Cindy was returned to a side street, one block away from the tennis club.

"I wanted to shoot them both right then and there, but I didn't have a rifle," Martin said, his eyes ablaze.

"I returned to the sleazy shit, fuck palace to ask the guy at the desk about my darling and my employee. Of course he didn't know anything. He hadn't seen anyone that fit my descriptions. The asshole says that folks come and go. He doesn't ask any questions, ain't none of his business. They pay cash and write down whatever names they please. A twenty dollar bill laid on the counter didn't jog his memory, but when I nearly crushed his trachea he seemed to recall a couple that had just left. They had been there once before—about a week ago."

Martin explained that he called Thornton and asked if there was anything new to report. The private investigator said that there was not, just a normal day for Cindy. When Martin arrived back home that evening, Cindy and Marcus were playing hide and seek in the living room. She reported that she had had a good workout on the courts and a pretty good massage afterward. Martin asked if Trip had taught her anything new.

She turned away and said he hadn't.

During supper and out of the blue, Martin asked if Cindy had ever heard of a private eye named Thomas Thornton.

She replied that she hadn't, and wanted to know

why he was asking. Why would she need to know a private investigator? she had asked. Her face had flushed, and she tried to nonchalantly attend to Marcus, wiping his mouth with her napkin.

Martin replied that there was no reason. He had just wondered if they had ever crossed paths.

That was the night the shit hit the fan. After Marcus went to bed, Martin confronted Cindy. He told her that he knew all about her "tennis lessons" with Trip. He told her that he had hired Thomas Thornton to spy on her and that he had times and places and photos of Cindy and Trip. Thornton had done a good job documenting the affair. Now, Martin demanded, Cindy must choose — stop seeing her cheating young lover, or give up her life with Marcus and Martin. The argument exploded, with Martin threatening the end of the marriage and Cindy crying and rebuking him for spending too much time away.

After arguing for an hour or more, Cindy had run to the bedroom screaming that she hated Martin and wished that she'd never met him. Martin retreated to his study, an emotional wreck. Anger and sadness gripped his heart like never before. Sometime before midnight, Cindy left the house with Marcus. At 12:15 a.m., the police rang the door bell and arrested Martin. The charge: assault. Cindy accused him of hitting her and threatening to kill her and Marcus.

Martin spent a long angry night in jail. Come morning he was released after his best friend posted bail. Now, Martin and his divorce attorney began to plan their attack. Martin detailed the events of the last few months and was assured that it would be an open and shut case. Martin then went to the bank to withdraw the cash for the attorney's retainer. But Cindy had beaten Martin to the bank. She had withdrawn all of their savings and had emptied their joint checking account. Furthermore, Cindy had also cancelled the credit cards. At the moment, Martin was penniless.

"I drove home fuming!" Martin stated through clenched teeth. "And guess what happened next, Mr. Fontaine?"

"I don't know Dr. Cochran, you tell me."

"Well, a black and white cop car was parked in my driveway. The cop tells me that Cindy has taken out a restraining order and that I can't go into my own house — that I must leave and never come back, that if I do I'll be arrested again."

"You're kiddin' me," I blurted out incredulously.

"No! The cheatin', theavin', lyin' bitch had me kicked out of my own home!"

"Damn," I nearly yelled. Then in almost a whisper, I said, "That sucks. That's cold. That would make *me* want to kill somebody."

Martin went on to tell me about the weeks following his eviction. They were pretty rough by anyone's standards. Immediately, he had to rearrange his finances — lots of paperwork. He had to get an apartment and all new household "shit." Then, for weeks, he had to constantly talk to his lawyer at $200 an hour. All communication with Cindy had to go through his and then her lawyer. He went without seeing Marcus for four weeks. And for at least one year, he had to purposely avoid any place that Cindy might be, so he didn't violate the restraining order. He lost many hours of work because of visits with his lawyer and two court appearances.

The one retaliatory shot he got at her was when he had the power, water, lawn service, and trash pickup cancelled, but that really was of little consolation. Five weeks after the breakup, Martin was arrested while trying to pick up Marcus for his scheduled biweekly visitation. Martin admitted he arrived a few minutes early, but swore that there were no threats made by him, no arguments. To him it was as though Cindy followed some list of dirty tricks aimed at pissing him off and destroying him.

"One time," he said angrily, "after a night shift, I went to get into my car only to discover it missing. I called hospital security and reported it stolen, then took a taxi back to my crappy little apartment. The next day, when I called the cops to check on the car, I was informed that it was in the police impound. It had been towed from in front of a fire hydrant a half block from the hospital, and I had been issued a hundred dollar fine. I also owed the wrecker service fifty bucks. Guess what, Pierre? That's not where I had parked it — and guess who had the spare set of keys?"

I just had to shake my head in disbelief as Cochran told his story. No wonder he went berserk. I disengaged from his stare and checked my watch.

"Wow, Martin, I can't believe how the time has flown! It's three forty," I said through the phone receiver, showing him my Timex. "We only have twenty minutes left, and there are so many questions that I want to ask."

Over the next few minutes, the convicted killer informed me of how Mr. Thornton met his end.

"I never let on to anyone that I knew Thornton and Cindy were screwing," he confessed. "So, I doubt he ever suspected that he was going to get it one day. The breakup was getting nastier, and I was sure to be impaled with the sharp end of a very shitty stick, so I made up my mind and formed a plan. People, get ready. You're all gonna pay — as we used to say. You're all gonna pay dearly!

"Thornton's part was a little more complicated," he continued, "'cause he would be out of town, but I knew where to find him. I knew he was scheduled for a spy conference in South Carolina. And I thought that maybe he would like to play a little tennis while he was there.

"The Columbia Chamber of Commerce gave me all of the info I needed," Martin said with a sadistic grin. "I knew where the conference was going to be held. I called and they gave me the schedule. I showed up in a little disguise, and followed my unfaithful employee to a café one evening after the conference. As he unlocked the rental car's door, I slipped a loop of piano wire over his head and tugged on the ends just enough to help him understand that he was to cooperate immediately.

"He drove. I sat in the back seat with the garrote in place, just loose enough to allow blood flow and breathing. While he drove, I whispered into his right ear the way the drill sergeants used to do it. I told him about the day I caught him with Cindy, and about what had happened to poor young Trip. He started to whimper and cry a little, so I tightened the wire to the point that he couldn't any more. It must have been a little too tight because he passed out for a minute and nearly wrecked the car. I had to grab the steering wheel and yank hard to keep from having a head-on with a semi.

"We went off the road into a field and finally stopped when Thornton come to and obeyed my command to stomp on the brakes. I couldn't help it. I freaked out a little and beat the piss out of the poor bastard. I knocked him out, tied his hands behind his back, and threw him onto the back seat. While he was out, I shoved a tennis ball in his mouth so he couldn't make a bunch of noise when he woke up. It was after midnight when I found the Greenfield Tennis Club. Thornton and I walked around for a while until I found the right tree. Then we sat under it while I made a little bargain with my private spy. If Thornton would tell me how Cindy knew how to act so fast and clean out my bank account and start destroying my career and reputation, I might let him live."

"I asked him who'd been helping her. It was pretty hard to understand what he said—you know, the tennis ball in his mouth and all—but I think he said it was one of her girlfriends and her lawyer. Well, Pierre, I don't doubt for a minute that that bull dyke, bitch lawyer put her up to some of the shit, but as sure as I'm dying today I'm certain that Thornton was a double agent, letting her know that I was wise to Tripper and that the marriage and her free lunch were about to end."

As I listened to Cochran ramble on, I continued to nod my head as I had been doing all along. My heart was about to pound out of my chest. In the next minute or so, I was going to hear a deathbed confession to murder.

"Pierre, I kinda hate it, but I lied," Cochran continued. "I had no intention of letting ole Thornton live. I was already armpit deep in this revenge thing, and no one was going to escape. I got right in his face. It was real dark, so I got in real close, our noses were touching. I wanted to see his eyes. I wanted to see the terror in them. So I whispered to him—real quiet like. I told him that I was going to kill him in a second and that the fucker had better say his prayers. I think he crapped his pants 'cause I suddenly smelled shit. He probably pissed too. I had him hog tied at that point, lying on his side. I gave him a couple of swift kicks to the balls and some time to suffer, then a fantastic elbow to the side of his head. God it hurt! My elbow was sore for a month. I murdered the freakin' bastard with my piano wire. Did you know, Pierre, that if you use a really thin one, and you snap it smartly, you can damn near cut their head off?

"He struggled and jumped around a little. Blood bubbled out of his mouth, around the tennis ball, and soaked his neck and shirt with great squirts. He was dead in a minute. And pulling him up in that tree was no easy job. I got bloody and nasty, and was damn near exhausted before I could get it right. I should have had him stand on something, with his head in the racquet, before I killed him. Woulda saved me a lot of trouble," Cochran said with a huge evil grin.

I sat paralyzed. Sweat dripped off of my forehead, and my heart had never beaten so fast. Martin had done it. He confessed to Thornton's murder and gave me all of the grizzly details. I sat staring at him for a moment, breathing hard like I had just pulled something heavy up into a tree.

Martin leaned back in the wooden chair with a satisfied smirk on his face. He looked like he could have been waiting on the bus. I recovered, and checked the time. Three minutes to go.

Oh no, I thought, *almost time*. My reporter's mind raced, realizing the immediacy of the moment. Then,

machine gun fashion, I peppered him with the most obvious questions. Rapidly, I implored, "But Martin, why
did Cindy have the affair? And why was she screwing
Thornton? And why did you kill Thornton instead of
the tennis pro?"

"Who said I didn't? Maybe they've just never
found young Trip. Maybe he went on a hike and just
never came back. And to answer the other question, I
don't know why the bitch needed to cheat. Maybe the
post-partum depression had her all twisted up, and she
needed some new dick to make her feel young and attractive again. I don't know."

The guard tapped Cochran on the shoulder, said
something, and held up two fingers. Two minutes to go,
I guessed. As Cochran acknowledged the guard, I
begged my final question. Martin's head was turned
slightly in the guard's direction when his ears processed
my words.

"And what happened to your son, Martin? You indicated that Cindy was responsible for his death."

His eyes returned from being focused over his right
shoulder. As they met mine, they were filled with rage
and the fires of a hundred Hells. For an instant, it
seemed like he might literally explode, spontaneously
combust. His neck veins bulged. His face grew crimson,
and those laser eyes ripped into my face. His agony was
palpable through the Plexiglas. I sat up and braced myself for some kind of nuclear powered onslaught or jet
powered scream. I wondered if he would tear at his
clothing or claw his face in a biblical display of grief. He
took a mighty breath, as though it was his last, and slowly exhaled. His shoulders went limp, and his face lost all
color and drooped. His eyes filled with sorrow, with

pain, with all of the sadness that the world had ever witnessed. They were vacant, haunted, exhausted. He was the most cheerless man I had ever seen. He stared in silence for a long moment. He did not answer.

Finally, after what seemed like forever, Martin tipped his face up. His eyes blazed again. He looked through the ceiling—all the way into the heavens and beyond. He smiled as though he saw the face of God welcoming him home, satisfaction surpassing description. Then, in a voice just above a whisper, with enraptured pleasure and lustful hope, he hissed, "Revenge is sweetest when served cold."

He relished the thought for a minute.

He sat back with a disconcerting smile and an impish twinkle in his insane eyes. He purred, "Pierre, I wish that we had more time. I'd love to tell you about some other interesting missions, but I've gotta go. The universe is calling. I must get ready to meet Jesus. Boy, this is surely going to be some kinda day!"

His eyes were on fire. He stood up and searched the ceiling as he mentioned Jesus, and he reached up high with his right hand as though reaching for deliverance, salvation, eternity. "You will come back later and see me die won't you, Pierre?"

I had stood when he did, then I froze when he asked me to return as a witness. Breathlessly, I replied, "Yes—of course, if you want me to—and if they'll let me. Of course, I will Martin."

The phone went silent. The guard took the receiver and cradled it.

As he turned to walk away, Martin lowered his right hand, reached out and placed his palm flat against the Plexiglas. His burning gaze softened, and he seemed to be searching my soul. Was he reaching out to me? I placed my palm against the window, mirroring his, and held it there until his dropped. During those brief moments, I felt as though I was his last connection with life, understanding, and forgiveness.

A sorrow came over me as I watched the former hero turn and march to his death. I felt choked up. My eyes began to fill with tears. He disappeared through the heavy metal door. It closed, and I wondered if I, too, had gone insane, crying for a murderous madman. I stood paralyzed and fought back the tears. I was confused, my senses rocked by the final moment's tenderness. What the hell was going on?

I was in a state of shock as I followed the prison guard through the hallway that had assaulted me earlier with its blinding polished floor and sonic-blast echoes. Admittedly, I was weak, a little nauseous. I lagged behind him a bit, lost deep in thought. Fortunately, the light of day and fresh air revived me. As I checked out, the guard returned my keys and belongings. He gruffly informed me that I must be inside the guard house before 5:10 p.m., or I would not be allowed to witness Cochran's execution as requested.

I grabbed a quick bite to eat, but kept it light in case my stomach revolted at six. I phoned Kelly and told her about the interview and the invitation to witness Dr. Cochran's last moments. Once again, she listened patiently and, once again, she was not happy. I had become too obsessed with this insane killer, she said, and, watching an execution was not only disgusting, but "way beyond bizarre." She insisted again that I drop the Cochran idea and return home immediately.

We ended the phone conversation at odds with each

other. She could not believe I was willing to risk my job and our relationship by befriending a maniac. I held fast to my belief that a great story would come out of my present efforts.

I made it back to the prison parking lot with a few minutes to spare. The scene had changed a great deal. Now, there were about a dozen uniformed officers standing watch prepared to squelch any trouble. CNN and a couple of news crews from other networks were filming opposing groups of demonstrators gathered together ready to assert their positions. One group wore matching tee shirts denouncing the death penalty, some carried placards. Another small crowd held signs that reminded us of the victim's rights and the loss to family members.

"An eye for an eye," I heard one of them tell a reporter. And though the scene was peaceful at the moment, I felt a definite energy and tension.

I showed my ID to the gatehouse guard and was herded into a small collection of folks detained inside the chain link tunnel leading into the prison. All eyes focused on me for a second, and the quiet murmur subsided momentarily as I took my place beside a gentleman who looked like a lawyer. I greeted him with a hushed "hello" and was repaid with a silent nod of his head. The buzz returned to its prior subdued volume.

I subtly peeked around and tried to guess which woman was the former Mrs. Martin Cochran. I knew that Cindy was present. Her name was on the sign in register. Could it be the one in the wheelchair? Was the wheelchair a result of Dr. Cochran's attack? The woman was facing away from the crowd and holding hands with an elderly lady. She seemed to be crying, her head jerking a bit as she quietly sniffled and used a wad of tissue to wipe her eyes, which were concealed behind large dark glasses. I tried to imagine what she must have been feeling. Hatred? Terror? Relief? How bizarre, attending the execution of your ex-lover, your ex-husband, your child's father, your torturer. *How brave she must be to come and face him one more time.* I wondered if I could do the same.

The march down the hallway past the visitation room was just as strange as before. The gleaming tile floor blinded me, and the echoes of footfalls pained my ears. But this time was also quite different. The loneliness and terror of journeying into the unknown was tempered by being part of a group. We all walked in silence. I was next to last in the procession.

As we passed the visitation room, I visualized the scene where Martin held his hand to the Plexiglas. A chill ran up and down my spine. A wave of vertigo and nausea caused me to stop and double over. I reached out and steadied myself against the wall momentarily. The guy behind actually grabbed my arm and asked if I was alright.

During that moment of wobbly consciousness, my mind zoomed through two daydreams at the same time. One vision had me walking down these hallways for the first time. I was being escorted by powerful, shadowy malevolent forces. My hands were restrained behind my back, tightly held by sharp, cold, steel bracelets that cut into my wrists, limiting circulation *and* thoughts of escape. My feet were connected by similar devices. Each stuttering step sounded a chain that dragged on the tile floor and then pulled taut to arrest my stride. It was my first day in prison!

The rest of my life would be spent behind these walls. The rest of my days would be shaped by these surroundings, limited by steel doors and concrete walls. The remainder of my earthly experience would be shared only with desperate, low-life criminals and hateful, malicious guards. There would be innumerable cell checks and constant anxiety. No rest. If I was lucky, there might be an occasional Sunday afternoon visit by a former friend or loved one.

Kelly's face flashed into focus. Tears streamed down her cheeks. I couldn't tell why she was crying. Was she weeping because she missed me? Or, had I hurt her, and prison was my punishment. The scene evaporated and left me depressed and puzzled.

A simultaneous vision had me coursing prison hallways for the final time — trudging down this very same passageway on my way to the death chamber, just as Martin would be doing in a few minutes. I envisioned leaving my cell, my home of umpteen years, for the last time, leaving behind unfinished writings, unfinished letters to loved ones. Leaving behind friends, even — those other prisoners on death row who may have become important to me, the guards who may have become my buddies, the voices and personalities that had partially defined my life in captivity.

I experienced the sinking, hopeless feeling of moving through space for the final time. My skin crawled and tingled as though I were struggling through electrified molasses, barely able to move, yet being prodded along by immutable forces that pushed and pulled at the same time. I felt both frozen and scorched. My head was about to explode. I saw the walls as though they were my final link with sanity, and the tile floor that I tread upon as my final connection to hope. It was all too bizarre.

My balance returned. I nodded thanks to my rescuer. My stomach was in knots and still threatening to revolt. I was sweating and apprehensive, but gathered my wits and courage and continued down the passageway another fifty feet, before turning left into the death chamber witness room. During those twenty five or so paces, I asked myself how Martin would be feeling as he took his final steps on Earth. Would he be terrified? Would he need to be prodded or dragged? Would his fractured mind realize the finality of the journey? Or would his insanity protect him? Had he found peace with God? What would his final words offer—a plea for forgiveness?

My heart stopped as we arrived at the viewing room door.

7

The End (Part II)

Walking into the execution viewing room made my head swim again. It was small and crowded with ancient, folding, metal chairs. The air was stagnant, as though there'd never been fresh air in the gray cement-block room. The chairs were arranged in three rows. The first one was three feet from a thick Plexiglas pane. It was opaque from age and scratches, six feet wide by four feet high. A heavy beige curtain prevented a view into the death chamber. The other rows offered little leg room, and all of the chairs butted up against each other. We'd be pressed against one another, shoulder to shoulder. There was a TV monitor, an audio speaker, and a clock hanging on the walls.

The woman in the wheelchair chose a space in the back row. Two chairs were folded and then leaned against the wall to give her room. Her friend sat beside her. I needed as much legroom as possible, but did not particularly want a front row seat. I got one anyway.

The guard who had escorted us stood in the doorway as we arranged ourselves. When we were all seated, he announced that the warden would be in to speak with us. He said we should make ourselves comfortable and keep the noise level down. At that point, everyone was silent, but momentarily several folks began to whisper and soon there were several hushed conversations. The voices seemed to fill up the room as though the chatter had become viscous. Each sound bounced around the concrete chamber, ricocheting off the walls before bumping into my eardrums like a flat basketball dribbled on a dirt court. The windowless room began to heat up, and I felt as though we'd soon use up all the oxygen. I stood, removed my sport coat, and inched as close to the doorway as possible.

The warden arrived in a few minutes and greeted us. He nodded toward the wheelchair lady and softly acknowledged her, saying, "Ms. Jenkins." He paused briefly, searching for the right words before continuing.

"I want to take a few moments to explain what's about to occur here this evening . . ." He paused again. Then, with authority, Warden Phillips said, "This evening the State of South Carolina will carry out the sentence that Dr. Martin Eugene Cochran received as punishment for the murder of Mr. Thomas Thornton. In a very few minutes, at six o'clock, the State of South Carolina will execute Dr. Cochran by lethal injection. I've been instructed to carry out this sentence in the most orderly and humane way possible and am charged with insuring that Martin Cochran shall not live beyond this evening unless he receives, from the Governor of South Carolina, a stay of execution, or a pardon for his crime."

The warden examined each face for any reaction to his statement. Finding none, he continued, "I am instructing each of you gathered here tonight as witnesses to the death of Dr. Cochran to behave in an orderly fashion. I will not tolerate any emotional displays. Anyone who cannot remain civil and respectful will be removed. Are we clear?"

The crowd chorused, "Yes sir," and we all nodded our heads. The warden stepped over to Cindy Jenkins

62

and held a brief whispered conversation. As they parted, I overheard her say, "Thank you," and that she would be alright. I imagined he'd expressed sorrow for her injuries and his concern for her wellbeing.

After the warden departed, everyone resumed their muted conversations. I stood close to the doorway, where the air was a bit less stale, and tried to strike up a conversation with the guard. He was a huge man, both in height and girth, and more interested in checking his watch than entertaining me. After an unanswered "how's it goin'?" and a "sure is hot in here," I gave up, sat in the worn-out metal chair where I had left my sport coat, and pondered on how Cindy Jenkins would react when the curtain opened and Martin came into view, strapped down and taking his last few breaths.

Would her blood run cold in fear of the maniac who'd terrorized her, or would it boil with rage, despising the madman who tortured her. Perhaps she would pity him and pray that God would be kind to the lunatic. Finally, I settled on a combination of fear and anger, with a soul wrenching dose of relief that Martin would no longer be able to terrorize her, and elation akin to the Rapture.

I studied her. She hid behind large, dark glasses, a victim. A victim of what I wasn't exactly sure. All I had learned so far was that Martin had disfigured her. Did he destroy her face? I envisioned a prize fighter's mug, badly beaten, forever swollen and scarred. Would Cindy have wide, pink welts replacing her china doll skin? She wore a high-collared blouse that concealed her neck. Scars there too? The only visible parts of her head were her nose, lips, and chin. She sported heavy makeup, including a generous application of lipstick, and reminded me of Yoko Ono.

She'd stopped crying and sat in the back with her supporters: an older couple and a woman who was fortyish. Her parents and sister? I wondered. I pitied her. Even though Martin's story had made her out to be a bitch, she didn't deserve to be mutilated. I wondered also, about the emotional scars that had tormented her through the years. How horribly sad: a blissful courtship and marriage unraveling to become a deranged, inescapable nightmare.

Even after the demon pays with his life the victim continues to suffer.

Martin planned it that way. He knew that each time Cindy looked into a mirror she'd be reminded of her tryst, be forced to relive her punishment. I prayed that she would grant me an interview.

I was snatched out of my daydream by the guard's voice, "Seats everyone, it's almost time. Now, I gotta remind ya'll that we'll have no outbursts. No wild emotional displays. That clear?"

A chorus of yeses followed. I checked my watch. Five till six.

Everyone took a seat and remained quiet. Shortly, two guys behind me began whispering. I caught bits of the conversation. They'd each been witnesses to prior executions, and were here to report on Martin's final moments. They fell silent when the drab curtain slid sideways, offering a view into the death chamber.

I sat motionless and held my breath. My spine tingled, and I gripped the bottom of my seat with both hands. A voice in my head screamed, "My God, it's really going to happen! The time has come! I'm going to watch a man die—no, be killed! Murdered. Not just some one. Not some nameless face on the television, but a person that I know, that I've spoken to, someone that I have a history with — Martin ."

I scanned the death chamber. It seemed sterile with only a cardiac monitor and two IV poles hinting at its purpose. The lights were brighter than anywhere else I had seen in the prison. The witnesses held their collective breath. The anticipation was palpable. A minute passed. Then, a doorway in the back left corner opened and a guard marched in pulling the foot end of a stretcher. Martin, already bound to the gurney, was wheeled in. The stretcher was locked into place. IV bags where hung on the waiting poles. Wires were snapped into a cable that led to the heart monitor. A small green light blinked in synchrony with a waveform on the screen. The display showed Martin's heart was beating sixty four times a minute — a normal, resting, relaxed, adult heart rate. His feet were bare, porcelain white, and bound to the table with thick, brown leather straps. Two more captured his thighs. The bonds around both wrists were tight as tourniquets, slowing blood flow, grossly engorging his hand veins and coloring the skin purple. The thickest strap was buckled across Martin's chest. From armpit to armpit, the bond ensured that its charge could not escape. Martin, however, didn't seem to be intimidated. He focused on the ceiling, as he was wheeled in and prepared for his final moments on earth.

One of the guards connected IV tubing to the existing lines. I guessed they were the ones that would carry the deadly drugs. An IV in each arm, Martin had said, would ensure the delivery of the poison. "If one IV line fails for some reason, the state will administer a second dose of death without missing a beat. I will definitely die today."

The chaplain followed the guards, and the warden entered the death chamber last. While Martin was being connected to the monitor and additional IV lines, the chaplain stood by his side and read from the Bible. Martin remained unperturbed, and seemed at peace. In a couple of minutes, Warden Phillips signaled to the guards to tilt the gurney. Martin's head was raised, allowing him a view of the witnesses through the scuffed Plexiglas that separated us. In that instant, I could not help but think of that pane as the river Styx. On one side, the Living, on the other, the Dead!

The warden asked Martin a question, then signaled for the microphone to be turned on. The speaker in our room crackled to life and fed us the sounds of the death chamber: the heart monitor's steady beeps; the chaplain's soft recital of Psalm 23 ("Yea though I walk through the valley of the shadow of death, I will fear no evil . . ."); the shuffling of leather shod feet preparing the stage, its star and his final act. I could hear my own pulse, jets of blood roaring past my eardrums through vessels that threatened to burst with each heartbeat. I could feel my neck hair snap to attention, and a tremor rip at my muscles. I could taste danger, doom, death.

The warden turned in our direction, searched his breast pocket, produced a small piece of paper, unfolded it, and addressed us.

"Ladies and gentlemen," he began, "citizens of the United States of America, we are assembled here, this evening, to carry out the directives of the Supreme Court of the great State of South Carolina pursuant to case number two zero one seven, the State versus Martin Eugene Cochran. Last evening, Mr. Cochran was read the court's directive: that he should be put to death by lethal injection this evening. We discussed the proceedings and I answered his questions. Barring a last minute order from our governor for a stay of execution, a pardon for his crime, or clemency, we will now discharge our duties. Mr. Cochran, do you have any last words?"

"Yes, I do warden."

Martin craned his neck, scanned our room with a malevolent glare, and settled on a point to my right. He drew a deep, deliberate breath and replied, "I would just like to say, sir, that in Deuteronomy, God says, 'See, I have set before you this day Life and Good and Death and Evil.' And in Leviticus, He says, 'He that killeth any man shall surely be put to death. In Revelations, it says, 'For true and righteous are His judgments; for He hath judged the great whore, which did corrupt the Earth with her fornication and hath avenged the blood of His servants at her hand.' "

The warden's face dropped. It flushed crimson. His posture changed from dutifully respectful to annoyed by Martin's language. Did he really call Cindy a whore and fornicator from his death bed?

"All right, Cochran, That's enough!" snapped Phillips, as he signaled for the microphone to be killed. But, before the switch could be flipped, Martin quickly repented and begged to quote Kahlil Gibran.

" 'Life and death are one, even as the river and the sea are one. For what is it to die but to stand naked in the wind and to melt into the sun? And what is it to cease breathing, but to free the breath from its restless tides that it may rise and expand and seek God unencumbered.' "

After a short silence, Martin closed his eyes and relaxed his neck. He laid his head back against the black plastic covered gurney and peacefully awaited death.

I, however, was anything but calm. The geysers in my ears reported more violently, more rapidly. I caught myself sitting on the edge of my chair, breathing heavily, wringing my hands and sweating as though I were the one connected to Death, and soon to meet my Maker. Time froze as I watched the killer's head sink and feet rise. The gurney returned to its horizontal position.

The warden checked his watch. He asked his assistant if there'd been any calls, checking on a last minute pardon from the governor. He inspected his watch again, whispered something to Martin, had the microphone turned off, and walked out of view.

Martin now commanded the stage. He was alone, in control. A faint smile proved to the audience that he was not worried. The mission had been accomplished; never mind the sacrifice, it was worth the consequences. Martin had won.

During the next few moments, I had a flash daydream. I envisioned a team of guards seated at the control panel, hidden from everyone's view, and each one with an unlit red button close at hand. And then, when signaled by the warden, they all pressed their switches in unison. Each button glowed red and indicated that the deadly solutions had been released into the main IV line. Next, I pictured the sequence of the chemicals' release: first the pentothal—count to forty-five; then pancuronium bromide; and, after a minute, the potassium chloride. Days ago I'd researched their effects. Sodium pentothal, modern miracle medicine now used as poison, would surge through Martin's veins, flooding his brain with deadly sleep, annihilating his consciousness, and ending his awareness in forty-five seconds. After his eyes closed for the last time, the pancuronium would course through Martin's bloodstream and attack his muscles. It would paralyze his diaphragm and prevent his breathing. No more oxygen for the murderer. Finally, the potassium chloride would bully its way to the heart and interrupt its electrical system. It would stop. Martin's heart would never beat again. It would ensure that the monster was dead.

The vision ended. Martin's final smile had become a satisfied smirk. In a moment, his eyes, which had been scanning the ceiling, closed permanently. I went stiff.

I watched without blinking, as though attempting to unravel a most impossible magic trick, trying to detect the very moment that the magician corrupted our senses. Watching for the line between life and death. I held my breath and counted absent mindedly.

His eyes have closed, now how long before the release of the paralytic and the heart stopping potassium chloride? How long will Martin just sleep before he is no more?

It seemed to take a long, long time. The wait was interminable, but it was probably only five minutes after his eyes closed that the heart monitor changed. The beeps sounded less frequently and the wave forms widened and flattened. Soon there was only a flat line. The blinking green light was replaced by a constant red light. The digital display of Martin's heart rate dropped to zero.

Martin Cochran was dead.

The witnesses breathed out all at once, as a unit, with relief. Satan could terrorize no more. Justice had been served.

I sat in amazement, numb. My mind went blank. A

flash grenade exploded. I was blinded. I tried to force my eyes to see through the brilliant white blob. I struggled to focus on the space beyond the partition, on the stretcher, the porcelain feet. I couldn't see his face. I couldn't see his expression. I could not see Martin.

Martin is dead, I told myself. It was hard to believe. I had spoken with him just two hours ago. Now, he was dead, killed before my very eyes. I had just witnessed a premeditated, calculated, scheduled murder. Our society, our government, even our religion sanctioned it, demanded it. "An eye for an eye!" Even Martin subscribed to the philosophy! My sight returned, slightly blurred by two small puddles. I quickly wiped them and stared at those porcelain feet, the lifeless form. Nothing moved.

Martin is dead.

A muffled sob broke the silence and soon several whispered conversations followed. The monitor's red light continued to scream out its message: He is dead, the criminal is dead, the killer has paid the price. After a couple of minutes a doctor entered the death chamber, listened to Martin's chest, and pronounced him dead. The curtain closed. I squirmed and looked around the room.

When the doctor pronounced the prisoner officially dead, the woman beside me quietly hissed, "Rot in hell, you sick bastard! I hope you burn forever."

"I hope he's tortured for eternity," said the guy beside her.

The couple turned out to be the daughter of the deceased, Mr. Thomas Thornton, and her husband. They'd come to witness Martin's reward for his heinous crimes. They asked me my relationship to Cochran, since they'd never seen me during any of the trials. In hushed tones we chatted during the few minutes it took for the warden to return to our room and debrief us. I told them that I was thinking of writing a story on the death penalty, which was *not* a total lie.

Suddenly, I realized that I didn't want them to think that I had any emotional involvement in this particular execution. I surprised myself. While I was reporting to them I discovered that I *did* have some emotional ties.

How can I sympathize with Martin? I've always sided with the victims and their families — it's only right. Murderers, criminals and demons don't deserve any consideration, no mercy. They've violated basic laws, respect, and decency. So, how can I feel any sympathy for Martin? He had cruelly tortured and killed this poor woman's father.

Warden Phillips returned, the room fell silent and he gave us his post execution spiel. On the way out of the room, the couple and I exchanged goodbyes and good lucks. I asked if they would consider a brief interview sometime.

"No!" they both replied in the same instant.

I respectfully nodded my head, half smiled, and motioned for them to go ahead of me. They declined. So, I tried to position myself to walk down the hallway with Ms. Jenkins.

Cindy Jenkins was rolled back to the guardhouse by her friends. I was close enough to hear the rhythmic *squeak, squeak, squeak* of her wheelchair's rubber tires intermixed with a parade of footfalls and all of the echoes, but I was unable to speak with her until we were bunched together in the guardhouse. I introduced myself and offered my sincere condolences regarding her injuries. The ex-wife of the freshly deceased, Dr.

Cochran, was not in any mood to meet new people and discuss her miserable past. I think I may have pressed her a bit too hard and pissed her off. But, I was feeling pressured myself. Here before me was the key to the whole bizarre story, the lynchpin in my investigation, the reason for Martin's metamorphosis from war hero and healer to maniacal killer. She dismissed me quickly, turning instead to her entourage, and collecting her valuables from the guard.

I felt deflated. Where could I go with the little information that I had. All was lost.

Martin was dead.

The story was dead.

8

Martin is Freed

Before Cindy could exit the guard shack, I boldly intercepted her and begged her for an interview. My mind raced to find some way to entice her, but I was drawing a blank. This wasn't a good time or place to ask for favors. She was obviously distraught. Why would she want to talk with anyone about her role in Martin's story? I could see she was about to give me an earful when the chaplain interrupted.

"Evening folks," he said loud enough to stop Cindy's response to my request.

"Please excuse me . . . Mr. Fontaine, I'm happy to have caught you before you left. I've got something for you. Martin asked me to give these to you." And he handed me several spiral-bound notebooks.

"Oh, thanks," I said accepting them and shaking his hand.

"What are those?" Ms. Jenkins demanded before I could ask the same question. "Martin's journals? Why the hell would he give them to *you*? Just exactly who *are* you, Mr. Fontaine? Some twisted pen pal, some ex-con buddy?"

"No, I'm not, Ms. Jenkins," I replied. "I'm a journalist who learned of Martin's impending execution six days ago. I talked with him a little — that's all."

"And I guess that you're going to write some sad story about poor Martin's downfall and how I did him wrong!"

"Well, no. Not exactly. I don't know what I'm going to do. Somehow, I got caught up in all of this and—"

Cindy interrupted and angrily spat, "Well, if you're going to read whatever crap is in those books and base a story on that, then you had better check *all* of the facts! And you'd better get them *all* right. He was a sick, evil maniac, not someone to be pitied. He got what he deserved. No, not really—he should've gotten worse. He should've been burned at the stake or tortured to death!"

(Miracle of miracles, here was my chance.)

"Well then, Ms. Jenkins would you consider telling me *your* side of the story? Would you call me sometime? My number is on my card, and I'd be very pleased to speak with you anytime you wish. I *do* want to get everything straight."

Before she could reply, the guards pressured us out of their post and into the parking lot, into blaring lights, microphones, and a cacophony of reporters, demonstrators, and no-nonsense law enforcers. Ms. Jenkins and friends pressed through the crowd with determination. Some reporters chased behind. She didn't answer any of their questions and she did not answer mine.

In the hotel room that night, I placed the notebooks on the small desk, then sat on the edge of the bed and considered them for a while. I didn't open them right away. To tell the truth, I was frightened by them. What kind of bizarre madness might be recorded there? Would Martin give up any more secrets? What else would he confess? Would I ever be the same once I'd read the pages of his demented mind?

After a while, I phoned Kelly. She couldn't believe that I had watched Martin's execution. She was disgusted and mad as hell. The tone and cadence of her voice did not conceal her anger. Once before, when we were newly married, she had severely scolded me with halting, choppy words spoken through clenched teeth. Every syllable was enunciated clearly and deliberately to emphasize the importance of each critical principle that I had failed to follow.

Now, I knew just how much trouble I was in for chasing after the Cochran story. She was furious. This time, instead of demanding I come home immediately, she said, "Don't bother to come home any time soon!" and she slammed down the phone. The line went dead. We were at a new low point in our relationship.

After the call, I sat on the edge of the bed for a long time, worrying about my marriage and replaying the day's events. I explored my feelings about breakups and divorce, Martin and Cindy. I thought about crimes and consequences, maniacs and victims. I investigated my beliefs about capital punishment. I thought about death and being the one awaiting execution. The walls closed in. The room became oppressive. I became restless, agitated. I needed air. I needed motion. I needed people.

I walked a few blocks to a tavern where there was noise, lights, laughter, and life. I had a few beers and exchanged banal repartee with a chain-smoking bartender and an old whore named Crystal for a couple of hours. We talked about the weather and complained about the government. We laughed at the drunk in the corner who fell out of his chair. We were trivial, base, shallow — simple little folks enjoying a night at the bar. My neck muscles relaxed and the knot in my stomach dissolved.

The hangover nearly crushed my skull during the predawn departure from Columbia, but it had faded into a dull ache by the time I landed in Dallas. While on the plane, in between cat naps, I couldn't stop replaying the eleven o'clock news coverage of Martin's execution: the pretty, blonde, thirty-something, anchor woman tightened her face as she moved from a feel good story about new funds for a local park to the "Top Story."

She sternly faced the camera and said, "And tonight we can all rest a little easier. As ordered by the United States District Court in Columbia, Dr. Martin Cochran was put to death this evening after spending nearly eleven years on Death Row. He was executed by lethal injection at the Broad River Correctional Institute in Columbia and pronounced dead at six nineteen PM. He was the first person to be put to death in South Carolina in over two years and the seventh to be executed in the U.S. this year. He was convicted of the 1995 murder of Thomas Thornton, a private investigator and a prior employee of the doctor. A Purple Heart recipient and Board Certified anesthesiologist, Cochran was also convicted of kidnapping and torturing his ex-wife in 1995. Additionally, he was suspected of killing his former wife's lover, whose body has never been found."

While the story was being reported, a photo of Martin was displayed. It was probably ten years old. He was thinner and without creases or gray hair, but his eyes were as insane and desperate as any could be. I thought of Charles Manson—madness on a monumental scale. After flashing Martin's photo, the camera presented a view of the prison: a concrete, impenetrable fortress —malevolent, fatal, topped with razor wire and snipers. Then, the broadcast showed the scene I had faced as I exited the guard house. There were armored police enforcing calm, demanding order. There were candle-wielding activists linked arm-in-arm, forming a peaceful chain opposing violence and the ultimate punishment. They were being confronted by a group of angry, vocal demonstrators supporting the State's decision to eliminate homicidal monsters. And there were news crews with high-definition cameras, halogen beams, and parabolic microphones, jockeying for position and the juiciest angle on the story.

Next, the camera focused on a woman in a wheelchair. She exited the guardhouse, pushed along by an elderly woman. Their rapid pace confirmed their desire to escape the man who was trailing her closely—it was me. I had the notebooks in my hand and a look of failure on my face. The camera followed the handicapped lady to her van. A caption under the scene read, "The former Mrs. Cochran." The caption and scene played as the reporter stated that the exterminated criminal had also been convicted of kidnapping and torturing his ex-wife. The audience was left to wonder what had happened to the poor wheelchair-bound woman. Was her paralysis a result of torture? The scene helped justify Martin's punishment. The images haunted me all the way to Dallas.

When I arrived home, I presented Kelly with a dozen roses, a bottle of our favorite Merlot, and a heartfelt apology. They did me no good. She dumped the flowers in the trash and didn't hear my full apology before she spat sharp criticisms of my disgusting behavior. We argued until the phone rang. It was Harry. He wanted the draft article on his desk by ten o'clock in the morning. As I repeated his demand and assured him that I'd be there at ten, Kelly stormed out of the house, slamming the door. I retreated to the study and tried to finish the piece. Unfortunately, Martin's notebooks insisted on whispering my name. Over and over they called — a siren's song, "Pierre, look at me, open me. I have something for you. I have the untold story. I have secrets, all the details. I hold your future, your magnum opus, your fortune!"

I hadn't opened the notebooks yet. As I said, I was kind of afraid of them. But now, in my own home, safe and secure, I gave in to the seductive call and opened the only one that had something else in it. It was an envelope with my name on it. Martin had written me a note. I was shocked.

In the moment, I felt honored. But after a beat, as reality settled in, I began to feel a sense of dread. In his final moments, Martin had written me a letter. Or was it something else? Perhaps a repeat of his last words, some instructions? I had to catch my breath. I put the envelope down and stared at my name written in the murderer's hand.

Would this be the deathbed apology his victims longed for? Would the note contain a confession to more atrocities? Would it mirror the letter from Dr. Jekyll to his attorney and friend Mr. Utterson explaining how the demon came to be, an account of his actions?

After a few agonizing moments, I snatched up the letter as if quickness would protect me from Satan's grip. I held it and tried to "feel" what was written inside. I swear it felt heavier than it should have. It felt like white hot hatred and evil. It felt like it should never be opened. It should be shredded and burned — immediately! But I did neither.

I carefully tore into the envelope and unfolded three

sheets of paper. On the first, I found that Martin had recorded the date and time in the upper right hand corner. He'd penned this just after we parted, one hour and fifty minutes before his death. A cold chill shook my entire body. Was I holding Pandora's box?

"*Pierre,*" the note began, "*did you watch me die? Was Cindy there? Did she cry for me . . . or for herself? Shame on me — that wasn't nice, now was it? I've won you know. She may have had the first laughs, some fun and games with little Tripster, but now I am free. I have stood naked in the wind. I have melted into the sun. My breath has been freed of its restless tides and by now I've met God unencumbered. I'm no longer a captive. I have prevailed, the mission was a glorious success — enemies vanquished, transgressors punished. Punished daily, forever! Even though I am dead. Can you imagine? There are things worse than death, you know — a wheelchair or a mirror . . . Tell her I said hi and that I've escaped my prison, my torment. My sentence was my ticket to freedom. The good people of South Carolina have put an end to my suffering. Pierre, talk to her for me, will you? Tell her I'll be seeing her soon. In some strange way I do miss her. Talk to her, Pierre, OK?*"

I put the letter down. This was too bizarre — talk about voices from the grave, the madman relishing his accomplishments, the psychotic fiend boasting of his triumphs over both his enemies and his own death. The letter went on, but I needed a break already. I turned to the Texas draft again and worked hard to make it interesting.

I stuck with it for an hour or so, but finally my courage returned and my curiosity dragged me back to the stack of notebooks. I left the letter where it was. With trepidation, I chose a journal from the middle of the pile. It had a yellow cover and was worn like all the rest. It was covered with graffiti and a single, expertly drawn eyeball. The eyeball was set in an eye socket, the upper lid partially covering the very top of the iris. It was drawn in blue ink and surrounded by a circle of flames, like I would draw the sun. It watched me as I studied it. There was hatred in its stare.

Carefully, I cracked open the binder to a random middle page. As I did, I felt like the guy who first un-rolled the Dead Sea Scrolls or maybe a sorcerer's appren-tice peeking into a forbidden volume of spells. I was apprehensive, cautious, *but* deliberate. I flashed on the myth: the world has never been the same since Pando-ra's Box was opened. How about *me* after reading *this*? I noticed my hand was shaking a little, my heart pound-ing. I admit I'm a wuss. I was breathing faster than I should have been.

Much to my relief, opening the killer's diary did not release Satan's minions or conjure up the boogyman. Instead, I was surprised to find a lengthy discourse:

"Time: what time? Time immemorial. Time immortal. No time. Marine Corps time. Jungle time. PRISON TIME. DEATH ROW TIME!! High Time. Before Time, Eternity, beyond Eternity. Time and Space. Einstein Time. All of the time, none of the time; never – always, who cares? Why are we obsessed with Time? We invented Time and NOW it's out of control! Time rules us! We ride Time. It's a giant wave, we're on the crest . . . (captured) hurled forward . . . (prisoners) floating, flying, in a desperate battle to keep pace with the power, the Energy. We fain control. Time flashes forward – only . . . – at light speed and it waits on no one (how cliché). Bend time, warp time, ignore TIME, make time, mark time . . . wait. STOP!

Todays' TIME I sat facing the corner of this cell, Lotus position, eyes closed at first — at attention yet disconnected from Self and Time. Timeless. Breathe deep, control, exhale slowly. Clear your mind; cleanse your soul.

Hours passed. Guards passed. Meals passed. Why am I here? And for how long? Does it matter? Do I matter? Does ANYTHING matter? When? Today? In two years, in one hundred? What about two thousand years? How few thoughts or actions have ever really mattered. My time in this cell really only matters to me. In no time I'll be forgotten. My actions may be remembered for a time, but . . .

TIME, consciousness and consequences. Does time matter without someone — a consciousness to witness its passage / progress. Consequences = a result of time? Without consequence how could you measure TIME. Would there be Time? If the sun did not rise each day, if we did not interrupt our present with sleep, would we be aware of the passage of time.

Time flies when you're having fun. Time crawls if you are bored. Our awareness of <u>change</u> gives TIME relevance. Time is a creation of man. We assign TIME its significance. We say that time began with the Big Bang, when things began to move, to change. Time doesn't exist without change, without space. Can anything exist without Time and Space? Anything with mass must involve space but what about an idea? It occupies only time. An idea, a thought, a melody takes up no space, but cannot exist without time. We are trapped in time. We are trapped by TIME. We have trapped ourselves. I am trapped in this cell, in time, by time, by my own hand. "Good times bad times you know I've had my share but my woman left home with a brown eyed man" . . . and I DID CARE! "I fell in love with a girl as sweet as could be, it only took a couple of days till she was rid of me . . . she swore that she would be all mine and love me to till the end" . . . but when she met *young Tripster I lost my BEST? FRIEND? . . . "OH GOOD TIMES BAD TIMES YOU KNOW I'VE HAD MY SHARE . . . I know what it means to be alone, I sure do wish I was at home . . . I don't care what the neighbors say" . . . and I hope Zeppelin doesn't mind me quoting and paraphrasing this way."*

I read the passage twice and reflected. All Martin really had was time, lots of time and nothing to do but write about it. I marveled at his genius and his madness. Then, I opened a different binder to somewhere in the middle. With this entry, instead of an obtuse discourse on some metaphysical subject and rock and roll quotes, Martin exposed his dark side.

"Torture is so easy — too easy, really! It's cheating. People are so weak, too afraid of Pain, and pain is so simple, so persuasive. The challenge is to find just the right balance between agony and death. Take your TIME. Slow, intermittent, Pain that's nearly intolerable. Broken fingers. Apprehension is almost as bad as the physical pain. The smell of the branding iron heating to glowing red. An experience that shoves our victim to the brink of sanity, to the edge of consciousness, a whisper away from death. Suspends the bastard over the ABYSS — dropping them into the fires of Hell, the flames scorching hair and blistering sensitive skin and then yanking them back, just in TIME — taunting them with a miniscule amount of HOPE while repeatedly abusing their senses with Satanic delights. Remorse, regret, submission, repentance, finally praying for an end, praying to DIE. Begging to die!!"

Wow! I couldn't believe what I'd just read. Only an evil, diabolical mind could think those thoughts. I shook my head and said out loud, "This is some sick stuff. He was definitely nuts," and I wondered if this was the mindset he had while torturing Cindy. Now, I was totally hooked. I'd met the bloodthirsty lunatic, talked to him, watched him die — pay for his sins. I'd seen some of his handy work: Cindy, the victim. Her scars, her torment, her tortured flesh hidden behind sunglasses, makeup, and scarves. Now, in the journals, I possessed the essence of the madman, his mind, his soul. Now, I could write something worthwhile, perhaps redeem my-self with Harry and maybe even with Kelly.

I was staring at the words *"praying to DIE. Begging to die!!"* with a lump in my throat and a full, hot feeling in my esophagus, when my wife banged on the study's door. It caught me by surprise. I jumped, slapped the notebook shut, and dropped it onto the floor. I felt silly.

Kelly had returned from a walk around the neigh-borhood, and was ready to talk. She handed me a glass of the Merlot I'd bought, and led me into the living room. She said that she was sorry for her rash behavior, and I accepted her apology. We drank a couple of glasses of wine and made small talk for a while, but before we retired, we discussed my shaky position at work. The conversation became a bit heated, and we went to bed irritated with each other.

The next couple of days were rocky at home *and* at work. I couldn't focus. My mind wandered to Martin's story a hundred times. The draft article was acceptable, but no work of art. I began a new assignment, and Har-ry put me on notice. Cuts are coming, he said. Shape up or ship out. And Kelly couldn't forgive or forget my ob-session with Dr. Cochran's gruesome tale. Within three months of Martin's death, thirteen years of marriage and thirteen years with the *Dallas Daily* came to an end.

During those months, I read through the eleven

notebooks. They were mostly filled with mundane daily events behind bars, but also contained Martin's memories, dreams, philosophies, poetry and, as you might expect, some wild, violent, unnerving rants against Cindy and her cohorts.

Also, Martin was a fair artist, sometimes decorating the margins and even full pages with images of various sorts. I lost count of how many times I had to put the books away. They weren't the modern incarnation of Pandora's Box, but they were filled with madness and evil, hatred, death, destruction, and revenge. I'm not sure what else escaped Pandora's grip. But unlike the myth, I didn't find Hope anywhere.

After reading some of the journal entries, I began to dream about either Martin and Cindy, or the other characters involved. Sometimes they'd play a small part in some innocuous fantasy, but occasionally I'd experience a full blown nightmare, complete with tearing at the linens, profuse sweating, mumbling in my sleep, or even awakening while screaming in terror. The visions could seem so real that I had a difficult time believing they weren't. Sometimes, I couldn't go back to sleep. Kelly was definitely not amused. And the final nail in our marriage's coffin was the result of one of my dreams.

Three months after Martin's execution, Cindy Jenkins called me. She had mulled over my request and decided that if I were to write anything about Martin, she wanted to have some input. She apologized for her rude behavior at the prison and went on to tell me a few things about Martin, their marriage, and the aftermath.

That night, I dreamed that I'd caught my wife cheating on me. I became incensed, and we argued violently.

She produced paperwork from the bank proving that all my life savings were now legally and irrevocably hers. She showed me explicit photos of her and her lover enjoying carnal pleasures that exceeded anything our marriage had offered. She laughed at me and evicted me from my own home, just as her lover drove up in my car.

Kelly awakened to the horror of me sitting on her chest choking her with both of my hands. I awoke when she smashed my face with her bony fist and bucked me off, throwing me to the floor. She was beyond livid. She was enraged. It was the end of our road.

Two days later she moved out.

9

Cindy's Story

A dozen years ago, after the attack and weeks of hospitalization in Albany, Cindy returned to Springfield to be close to her family while she rehabbed. Over the phone we agreed to meet in a public place. It would be less threatening.

I caught up with her in Washington Park one glorious autumn day. She and a friend were watching a couple of kids struggle with a Frisbee and a rambunctious Jack Russell Terrier. She wore a big floppy hat, a stylish scarf, and large, dark sunglasses. As I greeted her, she extended her left hand, and I noticed it was distorted. She kept her right hand fisted and tucked into her lap.

"Good afternoon, Ms. Jenkins. Thanks again for meeting with me. Wow, what a wonderful day. Look at all these autumn colors. It's not like this in Texas."

"Yes, Mr. Fontaine, it certainly is beautiful. I love maples the most—all the bright oranges and reds. And please call me Cindy. This is my friend, Anita."

"Hi, Anita," I said. "Pleased to meet you . . . and call me Pierre, if you don't mind."

"Okay," they both replied.

Anita asked, "Wanna move over there?" She pointed to a park bench drenched in sunshine. "You guys can talk, and I'll take a few laps around the park, get a little exercise."

We agreed. Anita pushed Cindy's wheelchair beside the bench, excused herself, and jogged off. We sat in silence for a minute. It was uncomfortable, my heart speeding up in anticipation of my first real question, but I didn't want to move too fast. I wanted to ease into the interview.

"So Cindy, is this were you grew up? In Springfield, I mean."

"Yeah, and I came back to be close to my parents. I needed their help and they were so wonderful."

"That's great. Are they still both alive?"

"No, Dad died six years ago, but Mom's still going strong. She lives two miles from here. I live around the corner — three blocks."

I nodded my head and smiled. "That's nice."

As she spoke, I noticed her enunciation was a bit flat, something like a speech impediment. I tried not to examine her face, but couldn't help it. I wondered what scars were hidden behind her oversized glasses and pancake makeup.

The conversation bogged down. We smiled at each other and pretended to focus on the beauty of nature and the park's activity. We treaded water, holding our breath, each silently waiting for the other to initiate the direction of the interview.

She spoke first.

With a one-hundred-and-eighty-degree turn in demeanor, Cindy almost barked, "I want those notebooks, Pierre!"

Her suddenness and attitude caught me by surprise.

"Oh! . . . Well, I'm sorry Cindy. I didn't bring them. And anyway I haven't had time to finish reading them."

"Well, I'm certain they're full of lies and pure crap. Martin was a lunatic! And I'm not about to have a book, or even one more newspaper article written about me without knowing what he said."

I was taken aback, and my heart sank. If this was her position, my trip to Springfield had been in vain and the interview that hadn't started was over. I could write something, maybe even a book without her side of the story, but it'd be far better to include it.

Then, I was silent for a few beats, the gears in my head turning. How should I respond? How could I entice her to give me an interview without meeting her demand? And I *hadn't* lied. I hadn't brought the diaries to Springfield.

Even with her eyes hidden behind her giant, dark glasses, I could feel her raging hot glare. It scorched my face and challenged my determination. Were we at an impasse? I held my tongue and studied her. She seemed intransigent. Were we finished?

"Well, Pierre?"

I didn't know what to say. So, I held my silence and raised my eyebrows in what I hoped would be a perplexed pleading expression.

"I don't know what to tell you," I answered. "I don't know what to say. I don't have them with me, and I really won't be finished with them for quite some time."

She studied on that, then said, "And anyway, why did Martin give 'em to you? Did he ask you to write something? Are you one of those gonzo sensationalist reporters who gets rich off of other people's stupidity and misfortunes? Are you just as twisted as he was?"

I stood up sharply, shook my head and declared, "No, no! I'm not one of *those* kind of reporters! I'd been researching a story on divorces of military personnel. Since he'd been in the Marines and his divorce ended in murder, I followed up on the story."

"Well, I'm *part* of that story. He wasn't just a murderer, he was a demon!"

"Yes, I understand. And I'd love to hear your side of it," I said softly. I didn't want to sound confrontational.

She watched me for a long moment. "Well what about copies?"

"That might work, Cindy, but like I said, I've only skimmed through them, and it seems like most of what's written isn't about you."

She held fast. She wanted to know what Martin had written about her.

I countered, "I understand, but wouldn't it be too painful, just stir up a host of bad memories? Some of it's really vicious."

"You're not my protector. I'll worry about me. I sincerely doubt that Martin's words can hurt me any worse than what he's already done."

She was probably right.

"I insist," she commanded, "or we're finished here."

"I really don't think it's a good idea, but I'll send them as soon as I get back. I promise."

"I'll hold you to that. What's your first question?"

I decided to start off with what I thought would be an easy question and one that hopefully wouldn't send Cindy or myself reeling.

"How did you and Martin meet?" I asked.

At first she seemed to inspect her lap. She spoke mechanically, emotionless. "It all started while I was vacationing with my parents on the Oregon coast. I'd been walking along the beach admiring the rugged beauty, when a jogger ran past. He had an athletic build and ran with strong, easy strides. A long while later, he ran past me again and turned into the path that led to the hotel where we were staying.

"That afternoon, as I was window shopping, a voice from behind said, 'Well, hello again!' It was the jogger from earlier. He complimented the ensemble I was looking at and asked if he could window shop with me. I was thrilled. He was tall and handsome. And he was pretty funny. He was older than me, obviously well educated, and somehow mysterious. We had dinner together that evening and shared a bottle of wine on the beach."

"Wow that sounds like a great opening to a romance novel."

"Or the twisted beginning to the worst horror movie you've ever lived."

I squirmed. How sad that such a wonderful beginning had such a horrible ending.

"At first," she continued, "he was a very sweet and romantic man, Pierre. We were together almost all the time when he wasn't at work. Before he became a partner in his practice, he had more time to spend with me, and we would go to the shore or go sailing. We went out at night to restaurants and clubs. Life was fun. Once he made partner, he had to be on a dozen committees. Sometimes he didn't come home until very late, or not at all if he was working the night shift. Then, when I had Marcus, we both became really busy."

"Lots of couples have kids and busy schedules, Cindy. Why'd you guys break up?"

She sat back in her wheelchair and examined me. While she studied me, I studied her. I took in how she sat, how she held her hands secretively and kept the scarf high on her neck. What all was she hiding?

"All right," she said after a brief silence, "how much of the story do you think you know?"

"I've read some of the news reports. Martin murdered Thornton, and you were kidnapped and assaulted." I was purposefully vague.

"What'd Martin say?"

"Honestly, Cindy, it was hard to tell what he was saying. He spoke in parables and quoted the Bible. I think he truly was insane. He talked about your affair and how you were going to pay dearly, but—"

"Yeah well, I doubt his version was anywhere close to the truth."

I shrugged my shoulders.

She continued. "I *did* have an affair and it wasn't right, but it wasn't criminal. And I have paid dearly! Martin's reaction was insane. Look what he did to me. He disfigured me, he scarred me for life. He butchered me. He made certain I'd never forget him and that I'd never attract anyone else." She removed her glasses. "My face is just the beginning of Martin's sadistic revenge. He made sure that I'd be as miserable as possible for the rest of my life."

I inspected Cindy's face. The dark glasses had hidden eyelids that didn't open all the way, concealing much of her beautiful blue eyes. Thick makeup made it hard to tell how much damage her face had suffered. But I could see her lips weren't right, and there was a scar on her left cheek. She pointed to her eyes and mouth with her left index finger. Her cerulean irises were bordered by upper lids that seemed to be too heavy; they were stuck at half mast. They didn't blink properly; only the bottom lids moved. Her lips were flat. They lacked the fullness her engagement photo had shown.

"The sadistic bastard cut off my lips and cut into my eyes. I can't even open them all the way. I've had nine plastic surgeries on my lips alone. What do you think about that? Don't ya think that should be enough?"

She offered her hands. They'd been devastated. Martin had been kind enough to leave both thumbs intact, but her right hand had only one finger — the middle one. Her left hand lacked a ring finger. I shook my head in disbelief, like a cartoon character. It was unbelievable. I couldn't take my eyes off her right hand, her bird finger. Martin had left his former sweetheart an inescapable message, one she'd have to face each and every day: "Fuck you!"

I was speechless. I sat back heavily on the park bench. Martin had proven to be more diabolical than I could've ever dreamed. He'd taken revenge to a new level.

"Oh my God, Cindy. That's horrible."

What else could he have done?

Cindy answered as though I had spoken the thought. "Yeah well, Martin wasn't going to let me off that easy — he severed my spine! Paralyzed me! And he cut off part of my scalp just like some blood thirsty savage from the Wild West! Now, surely Pierre, even Vlad the Impaler would've been happy with *that* much torture, but not Martin Cochran. Oh no! He went even further. It would've pleased the Marque de Sade. The sick bastard cut off my wedding-ring finger, sewed his wedding ring to it, shoved it into my vagina and sewed that shut!"

"My God!"

"Enough? No way! He poured acid into my bra

and underwear. It ate away at my skin for three days while I was tied up and unconscious."

She cried as she recounted her injuries. Her whole body shook with each thunderous sob. I was near tears myself.

"OH MY GOD!" I said louder than I meant to. "That's the most insane thing I've ever heard!"

For a moment I lost all professional objectivity. I was totally freaked out and angry as hell. Whatever sympathy, or empathy I'd felt towards Martin vanished. Cindy was right; her ex-lover deserved his fate. No, just as she had said, he deserved *worse* than death.

I thought I was prepared to witness Cindy's disfigurement and listen to her painful story because I had reread the news report of her being discovered in the van and had seen her in person a couple of months ago. I guessed she was paralyzed and her face marred, but my vague mental image didn't remotely compare to this. I felt her torment. I felt her agony.

"Holy mother of Jesus," I said softly. "What hell you've been through. I'm so sorry, Cindy. How have you survived?"

She didn't answer. We sat without speaking.

The silence was broken when Cindy almost whispered, "Pierre, I don't know how I've survived. A thousand times I wish I hadn't. Sometimes I wish that something in Martin's plan had gone terribly wrong and that I would've died in that van, or in the hospital. What I've gone through has been worse than death. I have paid dearly."

She had turned away from me as she spoke, but shortly regained her composure and soberly asked, "What else do you want to know? What else do you need for your book?"

I stared at her blankly. I couldn't answer. I'd pre-pared a bunch of questions, like any decent reporter, but I couldn't ask them now. It would be incredibly insensi-tive. So, we sat and watched the Frisbee kids and the dog.

When Anita trotted up and asked how things were going, Cindy said, "Okay."

But she didn't *look* okay, and I didn't feel so good myself. The breeze had picked up, and a chill blew in from the west. I grabbed onto that and said, "Hey, ya know it's getting late and a bit chilly. I do have some more questions, but can we stop for today? I'd love to take you two to dinner and talk about all this tomorrow."

Cindy declined dinner, but did agree to meet again the next day.

Prior to our second meeting, I literally practiced ask-ing the questions I planned to ask, and how to react to Cindy's distressing responses. I narrowed down the list to the most important inquiries, and watched myself in the bathroom mirror. I was determined to regain and maintain my professionalism, but I'd have to remove myself from emotional involvement if I wanted to be successful.

I arrived at Cindy's at noon. She'd invited me to her place. It was a cozy apartment, built to accommodate folks in wheelchairs. We chatted for almost three hours.

I began with: What happened to the marriage? Then followed with: What lead to the affair? What happened to their son, Marcus? Why'd Martin murder the private eye? I asked what she thought had driven her ex-husband to become a diabolical lunatic. Was there a history of mental illness? Had he ever been abusive before the divorce? And where had he learned about torture?

"I don't know how it happened, Pierre . . . and frankly, I was tired of thinking about it years ago. You'd think that I would've been happy with a new baby, a successful husband, and a lifestyle with lots of freedom. But somehow it wasn't enough. Somehow life became so complicated and depressing."

I shook my head and said nothing. I didn't want to interrupt her.

"It started out so innocent . . . just some tennis lessons, something to do to keep active, some time for myself, away from the baby and housework. Martin sensed that I wasn't as happy as I had been. He encouraged me to do more than just stay at home and take care of the baby. He suggested starting a new hobby, or taking some interesting classes at the college—maybe art or music. Finally, after a couple months, I relented. I told him I'd take a few tennis lessons. I'd already been playing a little bit with one of my girlfriends, and I had played a fair bit while growing up. I was pretty good already. So, I finally agreed that lessons might be a good way for me to get interested in things again—help me feel better, more alive."

Cindy paused. Then, while shaking her head back and forth, squeezed out, "How was I to know that the beginning of the end of my life would be tennis lessons?" She removed her glasses and turned away, with her hands over her eyes.

Momentarily, she pulled in a deep reinforcing breath, rearranged her posture, and, with conviction, said, "In a way, you could say that Martin was responsible for the affair. He loved the idea of the lessons. He even met Trip, and agreed he'd be a wonderful teacher. In my weaker moments, when I'm as angry and as low as possible, I do blame it all on Martin. But, in my heart, I know that's not true. I have to take responsibility for what I did with Trip. I was unfaithful. I ruined our marriage. I accept the blame, but the consequences far exceeded the crime."

I had to agree, and I told her so.

Following a short gap in the conversation, I straightened up in my seat, considered in a flash what her reaction might be, stole a shaky half breath, and, with trepidation, asked, "Will you tell me what happened to Marcus?"

Her response was not immediate.

The words circled, then coursed through my ears and bathed my brain with oily, soothing sympathy. I hoped Cindy didn't think I was using an old reporter's tactic—like I was Barbara Walters. I hoped she could see the concern I held for her. I wished I could fold her hands into mine, a show of compassion, an attempt to transfer some strength—enough strength to reveal the details of her young son's death.

She focused her gaze out the living room window. "Pierre, the truth is I was scared to death. So, I took Marcus and left town."

She stopped short, drew in a quick, defeated breath, and held it. She searched my eyes, then diverted her gaze to her lap and her tortured, mangled hands. Tears welled up and her chin trembled. She sniffled, stopped, and then steeled herself.

"I went to my aunt Celia's in Albany. I thought we'd be safe there. I didn't think he'd chase us all the way across the country. We could start all over and be happy again."

A prolonged silence overcame her and I waited. Her eyes darted back and forth as she focused on some plane —out there in space—questioning it, then examining it for answers, explanations. I could see that she was re-playing, in her mind, her decisions and their conse-quences.

"Take your time, Cindy," I offered.

She collapsed into the wheelchair, her face at first blank, lifeless. Then it became strained, flushed crim-son, and screwed into a horrid mask of agony and de-spair, a portrait of the misery and emptiness that can only be worn by the mother of a dead child. No tears fell yet. Had she long ago cried herself dry mourning Marcus' absence?

"It was all my fault," she continued. "I took my eye off of him for a second and then he was gone." She struggled to string the next words together, "We were at the park around the corner from Celia's house. Her son had been invited to a birthday party, and we tagged along. There were a bunch of kids . . . a dozen or so . . . running around and goofing off. Marcus was in a group, chasing Celia's dog and throwing her a ball." She stopped and shook her head as she said, "I took my eyes off of him for one second—*one* second! That's all it took for the ball to roll into the street and Marcus to run after it."

Her expression mutated into one of anger, furious at herself and the driver and the totally fucked up luck that left her divorced, disfigured, paralyzed, and childless.

"My son ran after the ball, even though we had talked about not doing that a million times. He ran right into the middle of the road, and was hit by a car. I whipped my head around when I heard the screeching tires and the horn blasting. I actually saw him being squashed beneath the car!

I screamed his name and ran as fast as I could. I screamed and screamed and scooped him up and held him in my arms. I screamed his name, but he was unconscious. Blood was pouring out of his mouth and ears. His head was like mush, and his beautiful little face was scraped beyond recognition. Blood bubbled from his mouth with every breath. His poor little arms were twisted and broken. It was so horrible! I cried and screamed, but he never answered . He was just barely breathing! Blood was gushing everywhere, and I felt like vomiting. People were running around trying to help, and, before I knew it, EMS arrived and took him. I was hysterical! My aunt tried to calm me down. They literally had to pry my baby out of my arms. Oh God! I was going crazy! They took him and whisked him off to the hospital."

Cindy wept bitterly. My eyes flooded, too.

"He died on the way to the emergency room. My baby was gone, dead." And she sobbed in great gasps and fits.

Now a chill electrified my spine, and the lump in my throat threatened to choke me to death. It seemed as if all of the blood had flowed into my feet, leaving my brain gasping for life. Her agony hung in the air for what seemed like eternity, then exploded like an atom bomb.

"Goddamn!" she shouted. "Goddamn you Martin Cochran! . . . Why? . . . I've asked myself that a million times." And she sobbed, her whole body quaking, a soul-wrenching, tortured wail.

Cindy bawled for only a minute or two, then wept softly into her disfigured hands, the only sounds coming from intermittent, spasmodic sniffles. I've never witnessed a lonelier, more heartbroken or heartbreaking image: the guilt-ridden, childless mother.

During the minutes that it took Cindy to compose herself, I searched my life experience library, trying to connect with her pain. I could understand it, of course, but nothing that I'd lived through could compare to her loss and sorrow. The best I could do was to remember how lost I felt when my mother died.

My father had passed years before, and I had no siblings. So, Mom and I became a team of sorts, sharing memories of Dad, memories of family life, vacations, tribulations, and accomplishments. We became best buddies. Our interests were similar, and we enjoyed each others' company. When she died suddenly from a massive stroke, I was devastated, my heart crushed. I was depressed for months.

I was in the middle of a little daydream, a memory: mom, Kelly and I sitting in Mom's kitchen, laughing about something, when Cindy broke the silence.

"I'm sorry, Pierre, I didn't mean to . . ." and her voice trailed off, as she lapsed into pensive silence. "I try not to think about all of the horrible things that've happened. Please, let's continue. What's your next question?"

"You said that you were scared to death, so you fled to Albany. What had happened? Why were you so frightened? Had Martin threatened you?"

"Well the first thing was that Martin exploded in the courtroom, when the judge read the final divorce decree giving me full custody of Marcus and ordering super-vised visitation. He actually jumped up and argued. His lawyer had to force him to sit down and be quiet. And the judge threatened him with jail time if he didn't be-have.

"As we were leaving the courtroom, Martin shot daggers at me. He looked like he wanted to kill me. He even mouthed something. I'm pretty sure he said I was going to pay dearly! I was so frightened that we stayed at my friend's house for three nights.

"Then, a few days after that, I couldn't get hold of Trip. He didn't answer his phone, and he wasn't at work. On the third day, I stopped by his house, but his van wasn't there and he didn't answer the door. He hadn't told me he was planning on going anywhere, so I got even more frightened. It wasn't like him at all, and he would *never* miss work. I thought something had to be wrong. Maybe he'd had a wreck or something. Maybe he was half dead in a ditch somewhere. Maybe Martin had killed him. So, I called his parents, and they said they hadn't heard from him either. They called the police.

"That evening the news reported that my lawyer had been in a severe wreck, and her car had exploded! Liz was in the hospital in critical condition. I had this terrible feeling that her wreck and Trip's disappearance were not coincidental.

"The next week the national news carried the story of Mr. Thornton's murder in South Carolina, and the lo-cal news said the police discovered Liz's car had been rigged with a bomb. So, it was really attempted murder. I totally freaked out! Martin was going to kill us all! I packed a couple of bags immediately, grabbed Marcus, and hit the road. I didn't know what I was going to do, or where we where going. But I sure wasn't staying in Tacoma one more day.

"I called my mom from Portland when I stopped for the night, and told her what was happening. I told her that I was definitely NOT coming home. I was too afraid that Martin would find me there. She suggested that I go to my aunt's house in Albany. Martin had never been there, and, hopefully, he wouldn't even remember her from our wedding. So, mom called Celia, and I drove there and stayed with her."

"How long were you in Albany before Marcus' accident?"

"We were there about a month, and I'd just gotten a job as a school counselor. It was only part time, but it paid enough for me to get a place of my own. Marcus could go to preschool on the same grounds, and I could see him throughout the day if I wanted.

"Anyway, about three weeks after school started, we went to the birthday party at the park, and that's when it happened." Cindy's voice trailed off as she finished the last sentence. Her face had fallen, along with all of her hopes and dreams. She was defeated and empty. I could feel the weight that hung around her heart.

She continued, "I was in my own place for only two weeks before the accident. I went back to Celia's when Marcus was killed. I was a total wreck. All I could do was cry and cry. I thought I'd go crazy. So, I stayed with her for company and moral support. Mom came up for three weeks, and I went back to work when she left."

"How do you think Martin found you?"

"I don't know, Pierre. I didn't tell anybody back in Tacoma where I was. And I'm certain that Mom didn't.

Martin was pretty smart though. You know, when I called Adrienne and told her about Marcus, she said she'd seen a newspaper article about the accident, and that Marcus had died in Albany. I'll bet Martin saw the same article."

We took a break. Cindy fixed us each a cup of jasmine tea, and offered cookies and nuts. Tea was enough for me. When we began again, I asked the rest of my prepared questions. She answered them and gave me the names of some former friends in Tacoma, along with those of a couple of doctors in Albany. I got everything on tape. All totaled, it was almost four hours.

Her cuckoo clock announced 3:00 p.m. We were both spent. She'd been on a roll, explaining why Thornton had been murdered, what had happened during her abduction, and how she thought Martin had learned torture in Vietnam.

"Cindy, it's late, but how 'bout a couple more questions, then we can call it quits?"

"All right."

"How'd you feel when you saw Martin strapped to the gurney in the death chamber?"

It caught her off guard. She sat up stiffly, and her face flushed crimson.

"I'm not sure. I hated the evil bastard, and I'm overjoyed that he's dead, but when I first saw him through the glass, strapped down, so pale and thin . . . I almost felt sorry for him. It's really strange. I was terrified of him. I was shaking and crying, and feeling like I was going to vomit. The hatred of a million years filled my heart, and I wanted to see him torn to pieces or burned alive. I wanted to gouge his eyes out! I wanted to kill him myself. You can't imagine how horrible it's been over the last dozen years. My life's not been life at all. It's been torture and misery—and Martin planned it that way."

Her eyes pooled with tears again, she slumped forward, cradling her face in ruined hands. She was pitiful.

And I wasn't feeling very good about myself. After all, I was the guy asking the questions that caused her pain to resurface. But I had two more queries.

"How do you feel now that Martin is dead?"

Through cupped hands, she spat hatefully, "Like I said, overjoyed. I'm thrilled that Satan can terrorize me no longer. But I wish there was something worse that he could've suffered!"

"I totally agree," I found myself saying. "Here's my final question, Cindy, what are your plans now?"

"Pierre, I don't have any plans. My child is dead. My life is torture. I'm a hideous wreck. I'm gonna sit in this miserable chair . . . all alone . . . till the day I die."

Cindy said those words with such force and conviction that I believed her. And that prospect was sadder than her disfigurement. I didn't know what to say. After searching her face for a few moments and feeling her certainty, I took both her hands in mine, squeezed them, and thanked her for her time. I offered to help her in any way I could.

I walked out silently. As I left, she sat stone faced and simply watched. I was shaken, but determined. I headed over to her mom's house.

Cindy's mother, Mrs. Catherine Ann Jenkins, recounted for me her memories of Cindy's courtship and early marriage, while we sat on her front porch, but not before she bristled. She stood up straight and menacing, like a cornered mother grizzly protecting her cub, and set her jaw as though it were a steel trap. She informed me, in no uncertain terms, that she was not happy to speak with me, *or* talk about Martin Cochran.

"I'll give you about ten minutes, Mr. Fontaine," she managed. "You see, I do not like reporters, and I hate Martin Cochran. I don't care about you or your book, and I'm overjoyed that Satan's spawn is dead. The only reason I'm going to talk to you is because my daughter asked me to. Now get on with it. You've got about eight minutes left."

I think she only allowed me seven. But, during the brief interview, she said that Cindy had been deeply in love with Martin during the early days, and they'd enjoyed a pleasant, busy life in Tacoma. They'd lived the kind of lifestyle that can be afforded by doctors and such —a big new house, new cars and well-to-do friends.

When Marcus was born, he was the brightest star on their horizon. They adored him, and made him the center of their universe. But, as time went on, Martin became more involved with his practice, and spent less time with the family. Soon, the doctor was spending too many hours at work and in meetings. Cindy felt abandoned, and became depressed. She took up tennis for exercise and as a form of therapy.

"Unfortunately, she and the tennis pro had an affair," Mrs. Jenkins lamented. "And of course, that was wrong. But she didn't deserve the punishment she received." Her eyes misted momentarily, but she quickly recovered and continued, "Mr. Fontaine, I don't know why you're interested in this awful story, or what you intend to write, and, really, I don't even care. But I will tell you that my Cindy was a beautiful girl who made a common mistake. And I guess that she should have paid for it in some way. But Martin Cochran took things way too far. That bastard was evil incarnate."

She focused her eyes on mine as though I was her mortal enemy, and she was about to cleave my head in half with her sword of retribution. After a beat, she continued, "And even though I was devastated when Marcus was killed, I'm overjoyed that he never had to see his mother like she is now, or have to know what a deranged maniac his father was." She stood, turned her back to me, and walked away. As she closed and deadbolted the front door, I heard her say, "Good day, Mr. Fontaine!"

I walked to my car in a bit of a daze. Cindy had told me her mother would be a tough case. She was tired of reporters, questions, answers, explanations, and the whole damn mess.

Back in the motel room, I referred to Cindy's list, and phoned her best friend from college. I had to leave a message, and was kind of relieved. After being bruised by Cindy's mom, I wasn't sure if I wanted to ask any more questions that day.

I sat in silence for a while, my mind drifting between Cindy's sad story and my own impending divorce.

Hours later, Cindy's college buddy returned my call and consented to meet me the next day.

At first, with a slight smile and a bit of twinkle in her eyes, she recalled her youthful friend, "Cindy was gorgeous, Pierre. She was fair skinned and petite. She had all the right curves in all the right places. The boys swarmed her, but she played hard to get. I'm pretty sure that she was still a virgin when she met 'him.' " She caught a deep breath, and then, with disgust, through gritted teeth and with hate-filled eyes, she spat out, "Martin Cochran." It was as though the very words tasted like filth. Still, she recalled how Cindy had excitedly told her about meeting Martin.

"She said he was a doctor—not only smart, but athletic too. She was crazy in love, absolutely giddy. She was as excited as a little teenage girl. They talked on the phone almost every day, and he came to see her a couple of times before Christmas break. She even spent a week with him during the break. That's when they got engaged."

Lisa looked away and grew quiet as if contemplating on how Cindy's life would've been infinitely better had she never met Martin.

"We stayed in touch pretty regularly for the first year or so after they got married. You know, she moved to Tacoma. Finally, I guess we both got so busy that we only talked once or twice a year. Even now that she's back—oh, maybe what . . . ten, twelve years—we still don't see each other very much. You know, I visited her and offered to help any way I could when she first came back to Springfield, but she'd changed. She was ashamed, I think, and deeply depressed for the longest time."

Ms. Stuart reminisced about shared college hijinks and about how she had received Marcus's birth announcement and how wonderfully Cindy's family had come to her aid after the brutal attack. She almost cried when she recalled her first visit with Cindy after the assault.

"My beautiful friend was unrecognizable! Her face was a patchwork of skin grafts and scars. She was paralyzed—in a wheelchair, with all her fingers cut off!"

Lisa's eyes glistened, and a single tear fell. It was as though she were speaking about her sister. "It was pitiful. She was hideous! That evil shit had mutilated and paralyzed my best friend. I wanted to kill him with my bare hands. I wanted to stab his eyes with a burning hot knife. I felt like torturing him in the worst ways imaginable. I cried for days. As you can see, I still cry, and I still hate him with my whole being."

As I headed down I-55 on my way back to Dallas, my mind boiled as it replayed the images painted during the three interviews: sparkling white wedding dresses and blood stained bandages; newlyweds intertwined, enraptured; and adulterers impassioned, frantic. I imagined adorable christening invitations and gut wrenching funeral announcements, innocent college antics, and a mortal struggle for survival.

I experienced the swollen heart elation of Marcus's birth and the blinding madness of betrayal. I envisioned Cindy's mom overjoyed that her little angel had married well and had produced a beautiful child, then disappointed after discovering the affair, and, finally, torn asunder when she learned of her grandchild's death and her daughter's assault.

I thought of Lisa, shocked by the sight of her mangled friend and brought to tears each time she thought of Cindy. And, of course, Cindy's description of her vicious attack and her first horrifying look into a mirror. The devastation wrought by Cindy's little tryst was unbelievable. And I felt terrible for dredging up painful memories.

That evening, I reviewed my notes and replayed the recording of Cindy describing her abduction and ordeal.

"He found out where I was living," Cindy reported angrily, "and he waited until I came out of the house to go to work. That's when he grabbed me. He nearly crushed my windpipe with one hand. With the other, he held a cloth over my mouth and nose. He pushed me to the ground and laid on top of me with my face in the dirt. When he finally let me breathe, I remember I took in a huge breath and tasted some horrible chemical. I guess it was ether. I breathed it in a few times before I passed out.

"The next thing I knew, I was tied up in the back of a car, on the floor. My mouth was taped shut, and tape was over my lips and around my jaw, up and down, so I couldn't open my mouth even a tiny bit. I'd never been so scared before. I didn't know what Martin was going to do, but I knew that I was in a lot of trouble. He was so strong and soooo angry! He didn't say a thing at first. We just drove and drove. It seemed that we were on a highway for a long time and then must've turned onto a gravel road. After what seemed like forever—and a million curves—we stopped. He got out and left me alone for a long time.

"The windows were up, and I couldn't hear anything from outside. I felt as though I was about to suffocate. My mind raced and imagined every sort of horrible form of death. Maybe, he would just leave me there and I would thirst to death in a few days.

"Finally, Martin opened the door. Cold fresh air rushed in, and I felt a glimmer of hope. *Maybe he's reconsidered*, I thought. *He's realized just how crazy this whole thing is.* But then, with one motion, he yanked me up off the floorboard and tossed me into the back of the van. It was Trip's van. I landed kinda on my face and side, and must've blacked out again, because the next thing I remember was seeing his face a couple of inches from mine. He was red hot mad, looking daggers at me. My mouth was still taped shut, so I couldn't scream. His nose almost touched mine as he said, 'Now you cheatin' little bitch—you're gonna pay. You're gonna pay dearly!'

"I was tied down on some kind of stretcher, and I couldn't move except for my middle. So I bucked and arched and hopped around as much as I could. And I screamed and screamed, but the tape wouldn't let any sound out, so I really didn't make any noise at all. I was terrified! Martin stood hunched over in the van beside me. He grinned as I struggled. He let me struggle and scream for what seemed like hours. Finally, I was exhausted and gave up. I closed my eyes and cried. Then, he sat down beside me and whispered into my ear, very calm, very clear, 'You're gonna pay! You're gonna pay dearly, you little slut. You fucking bitch. Do you hear me? Payback is a mother fucker! Payback—do you hear? You are going to rue the day you decided to cheat on me! You are gonna wish to hell that you never met me, or had my child, or took off with Marcus and let my child be killed.'

"I wanted to beg," continued Cindy. "I would've given him anything! I cried and cried and begged him to undo the tape so I could talk to him, so I could talk him out of whatever sick plan he had. But he wouldn't do it. He wouldn't. He just stared at me with white hot hatred in his eyes. His eyes were insane, Pierre. He'd definitely gone crazy. I'd never seen anybody like that before. I was sure he was going to kill me . . . but of course he didn't."

My notes indicated that Cindy was in tears and

shaking violently by this time. She was pale and slick with sweat. I recorded that I, too, was feeling the heat of the moment, the imminent danger, the anguish of impending doom.

On the recording, my voice cut in, "Let's take a break, Cindy."

After more jasmine tea, she took up the story where she'd left off.

"I knew Martin had been in the war and had killed before, but he never talked about it. He'd never acted violently, or even raised his voice, before the night he found out about Trip. Well, there was that time when two panhandlers wouldn't leave us alone on Waterfront Street. He gave 'em two bucks, but they wanted more and wouldn't go away. He finally yelled at 'em and punched the big one in the face."

"Sounds like he deserved it."

"Yeah, I guess. Anyway, in the van, he made sure I knew he was going to torture me. He held his huge Marine Corps knife to my throat and kept it there for a minute. Then he sharpened it slowly—inches away from my eyes. In fact, some of the filings fell into my eyes. He pulled and pushed it very slowly, very deliberately, back and forth across a grayish whet stone. I'll never forget that sound—*ssshhk ssshhk, ssshhk*. That was bad enough torture. Then he pushed the tip into my left lower eyelid—just enough to hurt, but not enough to put my eye out. He held it there and put his mouth to my ear. Again he whispered, 'Did I ever tell you what the gooks did to prisoners? They were very ingenious, very sadistic, very persuasive! They loved to cut you up, kill you slow, piece by piece. I f you knew anything, you'd give it up. They loved to rape and cut and burn you all at the same time.   They went insane while you screamed.'

" 'One of 'em would fuck you in the ass while another one would cut off your fingers, or shoot your hands!   They didn't care about information—they just wanted to get their rocks off.   Remember, I've got some experience myself and I've seen what they've left behind.   Did I ever tell ya about the guy we found after the VC were spooked and bugged out?'   He pressed the knife harder and harder as he talked, until I couldn't see out of that eye anymore.   I could feel blood dripping down the side of my face.   I wanted to die.   I begged God to kill me right then with a heart attack.   I held as still as I could and just barely breathed for fear of blinding myself.   He stopped talking, sat up to face me again, and pulled the knife across my cheek violently!   Blood poured down my face.   He roared with laughter.   I screamed with all my might.

"Then he said, 'You piece of shit little whore, you better not bleed to death!   I have big plans for you.   We're gonna have some kind of fun now.   Oh, you've never had *this* kind of fun before.   You think bangin' young Tripster was fun—you just wait.   Ya hear?   You just wait, my little Cindy.   Love of my life.   How did it go? Till death do us part?' "

I stopped the recording and sat back hard.   I had been blown away, absolutely astonished when Cindy had told me this during the interview, and even now, listening to it for a second time, I still couldn't believe my ears.   I had never heard anyone talk like that before.   I couldn't imagine a mind that depraved.   I couldn't conceive of being in Cindy's situation, and it was truly beyond belief that she could remember the words, the threats that Martin had used. During the interview, I had to sit back in my chair and hold onto the arms. My pulse raced and I remember taking deep breaths, almost gasping for air. I *felt* her terror. I *felt* her helplessness, her *hopelessness*. Adrenaline ruled. My fight or flight response was in full force. I would have run, but my legs felt like rubber at that moment. My God, I had thought. Martin. Manson. Satan.

The next voice on the tape was mine. "Oh my God, Cindy, how horrible! How'd you not drop dead right then?" I remember searching her for an answer and finding the panicked eyes of a victim about to suffer intense violence. She was *there*. She could see him with the knife and feel the blood streaming down her cheek. Her glasses were off, her pupils were blown. Her face was set—rigid, steely, prepared for impact. She was frozen in that awful memory.

I touched her arm and said, "Cindy! You're OK. It's over." Then, after a moment, "How can you remember all that?"

She whispered, "Pierre, I've had years of reliving this nightmare, this hell. I had to remember and retell every detail to the police and lawyers and juries. And I've relived the scenario a million times in my dreams."

She went on, "Martin waited a minute or so, then he pressed something on my face to stop the bleeding. He pressed hard for a minute then, he took something that was red hot, paraded it in front of my eyes. 'Crime and punishment,' he said. 'Crime and punishment.' I tried to move out of the way, but he held my head perfectly still by choking me to near unconsciousness, then mashed the searing metal into the knife wound. I passed out."

I paused the tape again, and scribbled in my notepad, "*Crime and Punishment*." I wanted to check that topic in Martin's notebooks. I recalled he'd filled a couple of pages with the subject.

I restarted the tape recorder. "When I woke up," Cindy continued, "Martin was calling my name. He was saying, 'Cindy, Cindy, Cindy wake up. Wake up! You don't want to miss this. We're just getting started. You gotta wake up so ya don't miss anything.' He had my hands tied to the sides of the cot. I couldn't move them, but I could grip and make a fist. So, when he tried to get my fingers I did my best to scratch him and dig my fingernails into his flesh and ball up my fists. But finally, he won. He said, 'I remember how proud you were of your beautiful nails. You took such care to file them just right and to paint them just so. You spent so much time on them. Well, lucky you — after today you'll get half-off manicures.'

"Pierre, I thought I'd go insane right then. I thought he was going to cut off my fingers with that huge knife. I screamed and screamed. I bucked and resisted as much as I could. He grabbed my fingers, but couldn't hold them still enough to do whatever. So he bent a couple of them back until they snapped. My God, the pain was unimaginable. I screamed until I could taste blood in the back of my throat. I guess I ruptured my vocal cords, and then I nearly passed out again. Everything went black for a second and then spun like I was on a carnival ride. I wanted to vomit. I wretched a couple of times. Martin snatched the tape off my mouth and jerked my head to the side while he wailed with laughter. 'Don't you puke and aspirate you rancid slimy cunt. You know it's against the rules to die! You gotta suffer, man. You gotta know how it feels to suffer! How it feels to have everything that you've busted your ass for go down the drain, be taken from you. You gotta live some hell. Oh, and Cindy—you ARE going to live some hell.' He burst out laughing again and plunged a needle into my arm. I screamed as loud as I could, but nothing came out. In seconds I saw wild colors and shapes moving around the van.

"Next thing I knew, I woke up. I guess I was out for a while, because when I came to, I was on my side. Still tied down, but now curled up in a ball.

"Martin was doing something to my back. I couldn't tell if he was stabbing me or burning me. The pain was terrible. It felt deep and dull and sharp, all at the same time. I wiggled as best I could, and he didn't try to stop me. He just laughed a sadistic little laugh. And then, he suddenly yanked my hair back so that I was facing him. His eyes burned with hatred. He said, 'I might could've gotten over you fucking around and maybe even ruining my career, my life, but I just can't get over losing Marcus, and I hold you totally responsible.'

Cindy went on, "Sadness replaced hatred and I think he almost cried, Pierre. I wanted to explain that it was a horrible accident, that Marcus could've been killed just as easily back in Tacoma. I wanted to remind him that Marcus had been *my* child too—that I was just as devastated. I was his *mother!* I had carried him in my belly." Tears streamed down Cindy's face now like an open faucet, washing away her heavy makeup. "He'd been a *part* of me," she barely managed through spasmodic sobs. "But Martin had re-taped my mouth, and I couldn't say a word."

I turned off the tape recorder and sat in silence for a few minutes, pondering. My chest was heavy. I was amazed and sickened. Just like Cindy's mother had said: this was an awful story. And I remember asking myself aloud, "Why are you writing about this, Pierre?" I shook my head in disbelief. *Am I just as depraved as Martin? Am I pandering to sensationalism, our base, and vulgar curiosity? Why should I want to expose the details of Martin's diabolical revenge and the embarrassing humiliation that Cindy was been forced to suffer? Why would anyone want to read about this demented saga?*

I unplugged the recorder and put away all my notes. I had to stop for now, but I couldn't clear my mind of the question: Why write about Martin and Cindy?

10

Crime and Punishment

It took me a couple of days before I could return to the tape recorder and notes. I had to deal with my own divorce: phone calls, phone tag, lawyer appointments, and arguments. How should we divvy up my 401K and our property? There were interminable hours spent sitting in lawyers' offices and conference rooms with a mediator, my blood boiling, listening to lies. Our lawyers played word games and debated the finer points of asset dispersal, like splitting the spoons and forks evenly. And, at two hundred and fifty dollars an hour, I began to understand why people go nuts during a divorce.

Also, I had to write an article for a magazine. Since being fired, I'd been picking up small jobs to bring in some much needed cash. But finally, I sat down again and picked up where I had left off.

First I considered the question of why write about Martin and Cindy. I didn't come to any earth shattering conclusions, so I just forged ahead.

Martin's words to Cindy, *"Crime and Punishment,"* had been echoing in my head so I flipped through Martin's notebooks until I found the relevant pages. About halfway through a worn, blue spiral notebook, Martin had doodled in the top margin a knife, a flame, a syringe and a hangman's noose. Below them, he printed in large bold letters:

CRIME and PUNISHMENT. And for two pages he explored the subject.

He began:

CRIME — an act having injurious consequences. Punishment — retribution! . . . But who decides which acts are crimes?? And who declares the appropriate punishment?? The Bible gives plenty of examples of deeds (sins) worthy of punishment and mostly they are punished by death. GENESIS . . . He that smiteth a man — or his father or mother — or curseth his father OR steal a man and sell him shall be put to DEATH! Even a poor ox will be stoned and put to death if he fucks up. And, of course, if you lie with an animal or another man or screw another man's wife, or kill a man, YOU are going to be put to DEATH.

A circle was drawn around *screw another man's wife*, and a line connected it to two other circles drawn below. What began as a simple circling of initials had been transformed into a doodle. The initials TT were ensnared in a hangman's noose and TJ was surrounded by a ring of flames. Thomas Thornton? Trip Johnson? A confession? A satisfying reminder? Evidence? Martin had already been sentenced to death so he probably didn't care what anyone might think.

He went on with a review of how laws began. He wrote a few thoughts about the Codex Hammurabi, the Ten Commandments and Roman laws:

But who put these guys in charge? THEY TOOK CHARGE. They were already in power or took control by force (KILLING PEOPLE?) and then decided what was good, what was bad and what would happen to those who defied THE RULES. Their rules, the ones that they just made up! The ones that supported their ideas. The ones that protected their world . . . This is MY world said the king. I'll tell you what's right and what's wrong. Screw up and you'll receive the punishment I decide. . . . Killing is OK if the top dog says

117

it is. *Killing is a sin unless it's used as a punishment against a villain. The United States Government can kill ya if they want, THE PEOPLE of South Carolina can murder you if they want to – 12 people decide. What about MY world? Why can't I decide? MAYBE . . . if someone fucks you over you should have the right to fuck them up. Maybe you shouldn't always kill the transgressor, maybe just mess them up. Life in Prison don't need to have walls! Don't need no razor wire! Don't need no guards!*

Crime – crime – CRIME! It's everywhere. In the home. On the street. In this here PRISON. In the bitch's head. Her crimes are: betrayal, theft, lies!!! Did she kill my son? MY SON.

A decent likeness of Cindy with a forked tongue and devil horns decorated the right hand margin:

What should the punishment be for the golden haired Angel, sent from above, who hath destroyed everything I made, who hath destroyed my home, my job, my family, my child, our plans, my FAITH? HOPE? Wouldn't Hammurabi consider the CRIME and kill her instantly? Probably. Would Deuteronomy sentence the adulterers to death. I think so. Would Solomon shake his head in disgust and split everything 50/50? No. It's all hers sayeth the system. Is a child property? If a wife ruineth a husband's life wouldn't it be fair that he should ruineth hers . . . 'Instant karma's gonna get cha.' (JL)

What is my crime? What is my punishment?

LIFE CAN BE WORSE THAN DEATH! . . . death = freedom . . .

". . . I'm not frightened of dying – any time will do, I don't mind. Why should I be frightened of dying? I see no reason for it. You've got to go sometime." PINK FLOYD

My crime – Guilty of working hard. Providing a sweet lifestyle.

My Punishment: disrespect.

Reading Martin's notes sent a twinge of sympathy through my nervous system; it pinched my heart. He had some valid points, but I truly believe that Cindy's punishment far exceeded her crime. I listened to the remainder of Cindy's interview and had another look at my notes. Cindy had just recalled waking up to discover that Martin was doing something to her back and that tape had been reapplied to her mouth.

"He had pulled my hair so hard and jerked my neck around so violently I thought my neck was broken. He got right in my face and said, 'You killed my son, Cindy. You stole my son. You kidnapped my boy and got him killed! I'll never forgive you for that. And now, you're gonna pay. You like screwing around so much? Well you're gonna screw yourself! Just wait! As long as you live you will never forget your fuck up.' "

Cindy continued, "He let go of my hair, and my head flopped down, and the next thing I remember is waking up, all tied down, in agony and screaming. Bandages were all over my face. I must've screamed for hours before someone finally heard me and rescued me.

"I remember someone trying to open the van doors, finally breaking out a window and cutting my hands free. I'll never forget what a relief I felt. I was alive! I was free! The nightmare was over! I remember being rushed into the hospital, asked a million questions, and being examined by doctors and nurses. I remember their expressions when they removed the bandages from my face. They were horrified! That look of shock and pity is the last memory I have until, sometime – a of couple days later—I woke up in a hospital bed. Mother was beside me."

I turned the recorder off again, closed my eyes, and tried to imagine what it was like waking up in that van in agony, filled with terror. I studied on what it must have felt like for Cindy's mom, alone, on duty at her daughter's side. I tried to put myself in Martin's place: betrayed, grieving, infuriated.

The rest of the interview dealt with Cindy's hospitalizations, numerous surgeries, intensive psychological therapy, and rehab. It was all miserable and heartbreaking. The many weeks and months spent healing would have—as the worn out saying goes—"tried the patience of Job." I planned to listen to that part later. First, I wanted to read the Albany police reports and speak with any witnesses of Cindy's rescue.

I flew to Albany and checked in at police headquarters.

"Detective Dave Reynolds and Lieutenant "Scooter" Buyes had worked Cindy's case. They'd be the guys to talk to," said Police Chief T. Smart. "Unfortunately, Dave Reynolds is dead. He passed a couple of years after the Jenkins case," reported the Chief with sadness.

"We were good buddies, even though he was quite a bit older than me. You see, Dave retired after thirty-eight years on the force. Lots of honors. Yep, he was a hell of a detective, could sniff out clues like a bloodhound—and fearless too! I saw him in action several times. Uh huh."

Smart nodded his head up and down, pursed his lips, and continued, "His bravery is what got him killed. See, he walked into this convenience store just as some punk was robbing it. The clerk was being held by his collar, the pistol right between his eyes. Reynolds drew on the perp, but he was too slow I guess. He took one in the chest and one in the leg, died on the way to the hospital. He did get off a couple of shots, saved the clerk's life."

Chief Smart cut his eyes and studied the desk in front of him. In a few seconds he went on, "And, Mr. Fontaine, you might not get much outta Scooter. He's been dying of throat cancer for a few years. I'm not sure he's still alive, and, if he is, I don't know if he can still talk."

I found Scooter Buyes at home. He'd endured his sixth operation for cancer, and been out of the hospital for two days. His wife reluctantly let me in, and he did his best to answer my questions. The interview was difficult. Not only did he look like death, pallid and frail, but he was tough to understand. He "talked" with the aid of one of those vibrating microphones you press against your throat after your larynx has been removed, and he breathed through a hole in his neck called a tracheostomy. His sentences were choppy. He'd take a sonorous breath in through the blowhole, "say" four or five words, vacuum in three fresh breaths with his ruined lungs, say another few words, and finish his thought as quickly as possible. And he still smoked by holding the butt close to the trach and inhaling. What a sight. He explained that since he was almost dead, he may as well smoke to his heart's content.

"I remember," he said, sounding like a rusty, soulless kazoo, "gruesome . . . like some mad scientist." He breathed heavily and took a drag from his cigarette. "A portable operating room . . . all sorts of medical equipment . . . empty vials of drugs."

He rested and breathed; I waited patiently. His wife watched from the kitchen door.

"Flashlights on the ceiling . . . Army cot, tape, blood everywhere." Another rest and a coughing fit. "Even antibiotic ointment . . . he wanted her to live." A new cigarette and gasping breaths. "Guards compromised the scene . . . everybody was freaking out."

More coughing and gasping. Mrs. Buyes marched over, snuffed the cigarette and fitted an oxygen mask over Scooter's trach hole. He slapped at her hands, but didn't resist much. While he caught his breath, she told the rest of the story. "They couldn't interview the woman for several days—she was nearly dead. When she *could* talk, she said her husband had kidnapped and tortured her for having an affair with the tennis pro."

With his mechanical voice near exhaustion, Scooter finished with, "Never seen anything like it . . . He cut her up . . . *and* sewed her up . . . Parked at the hospital . . . so she'd live."

I thought that the last sentence was going to kill Detective Buyes. He dropped his vibraphone into his lap, took several deep breaths, and waved me off.

"Check the records," he mouthed to me.

I politely shook his hand and exited.

I *did* check the records, but it took some doing. My reporter ID, secreted away before I was fired from the *Dallas Daily*, didn't hold as much sway with the "Evidence and Archives" desk sergeant as it did with Chief Smart. It took an hour to wade through the proverbial, mind-numbing "red tape" and jump through the universally dreaded bureaucratic "hoops." I think the sergeant really enjoyed watching me negotiate the process. His eyes twinkled and he gave me a crooked, devilish smile as he handed me a pile of papers to fill out. And I heard him snicker when the magistrate's secretary, speaking via the intercom, gave me a hard time.

Finally, just before closing time, I made it into the evidence catacombs. A poorly lit warehouse filled with endless rows of open shelves, straining from the weight of hundreds of boxes, floor to ceiling, each marked with case numbers, dates, and names. The room smelled musty like earth and sweat. I imagined the boxes filled with all types of criminal tools, implements of theft, death and destruction, and misery. I pictured all sorts of murder weapons: switchblades; butcher knives; stolen pistols and hunting rifles; axes; Billy clubs; garrotes; and poisons. And I imagined the damning evidence, tagged and catalogued: spent bullet casings; blood-stained clothes; ballistics reports and bullet riddled skulls; broken bones; handcuffs; duct tape; finger print comparisons and DNA reports; crime-scene photos and signed confessions.

What I found were four boxes marked "STATE VS M. COCHRAN / 75211:87." I hauled them up to the viewing room, immediately adjacent to the desk sergeant's post. It was much better illuminated, and held a large, grimy oak table, a couple of well-worn wooden chairs, and, resting in a corner, some old metal folding chairs. Also, there were five obvious cameras, one in each corner and one directly above the table.

Sergeant "What's his name" — I never caught it, because his name tag was missing, and he stuttered so severely that I quit listening anyway — cupped his chin in his palm and diligently watched me as I opened the box marked Number One. It contained the "Evidence Catalogue" sheet and some other items. The catalogue listed, in alphabetical order, all of the items in the boxes along with the quantity, or size of each if applicable. I made notes and copied some of the evidence notations, as I removed, studied, and then replaced the damning items.

The sergeant's shift ended at 6:00 p.m., and so I had to go, but I returned the next day, bright and early. Apparently, he was not a morning person, his sense of humor unaccustomed to opening-bell visitors. He sneered as I greeted him with a chipper, "Good morning Sergeant." I signed in and began where I left off. Most of the stuff I found in the boxes — medical equipment, bandages and such — had already been described briefly by Det. Buyes. Yet, there were still some disturbing surprises. The most gruesome of which was a large Ziploc baggie containing what appeared to be a strip of hairy leather. An index card in the sealed bag read: "PORTION OF SCALP. APPROX. 3.7 cm X 5.1 cm."

When the words registered in my brain, I gasped, dropped the bag, and scooted back my chair abruptly. Once again, Martin's demented deeds had knocked the wind out of me. What other surprises would he have for me?

Sergeant "What's his name" rushed into the room and inquired as to the commotion. He saw the baggie and then told me that he had heard about the Indian-style scalping, but had never seen the evidence. (Of course, it took him ten minutes to spit out the sentence.)

Other evidence included: an ice pick; several plastic zip ties; an empty can of Naval Jelly; two sections of the *Tacoma Times* (each with a different date); another baggie of curled "leather" (dried skin); and horrifying Polaroids of Cindy's wounds photographed in the emergency room, including three different views of her disarticulated left ring finger—now slimy black—in the early stages of rotting and still with Martin's gold band attached.

Documents from police investigators, the forensic pathologist, and emergency room doctors, explained that the second Ziploc of dried skin had once been Cindy's lips. The zip ties had been used as tourniquets around Cindy's fingers—impeding blood supply for days and necessitating amputations. The ring finger was discovered when a nurse couldn't place a urinary catheter in Cindy's vagina, because it had been sewn shut. The Naval Jelly—phosphoric acid—had been spread onto her breasts and genitals, dissolving her skin. And the ice pick had probably been used to puncture her back, scramble her spinal cord, and cause permanent paralysis from the waist down.

I was glad to be sitting, as I examined the photographs and read through the details of the gruesome crime scene. It was totally insane. Martin was a madman, undeniably evil.

I spent a couple of hours sifting through the evidence boxes and making notes. When I finished, the sergeant inspected the boxes and made certain that each item catalogued remained present. He released me, and I proceeded to the Court Records Library.

The record of case 75211:87, The State vs. Martin Cochran, had filled two hundred and sixteen typewritten pages, but had been converted to a little-more-than-nine-hundred-kilobytes file. This included all of the testimony presented in court, a description of the evidence, the comments of the Court, and its resulting sentence.

It took hours of reading and then piecing together to

get the full story. The State presented a scenario that echoed what Cindy had told me. Plus, the authorities had discovered that Martin had used the anesthetic drugs: sodium pentothal and ketamine, to keep Cindy unconscious during most of her time in the van.

On December 14, hospital security guard, Ralph S. Morgan responded to a commotion inside a van parked in the loading dock area of St. Peter's Hospital. He found Cindy in the van, securely fastened to an Army cot, covered in dried blood and stained bandages. She was hysterical. Morgan called for help. Cindy was rushed into the Emergency Room then the ICU, where she was treated for the wounds she had described to me earlier.

Documents described what copies of the Polaroids showed: the crown of her head missing a swath of hair and scalp; her eyes swollen shut, the lids black and blue; a deep laceration on her left cheek; and her lips missing. Cindy's teeth were exposed. There was no way to cover them, since no tissue remained. She seemed to leer at the photographer like the skull pictured on a pirate's flag. Dried black blood filled the spaces in between her teeth.

Other photos showed her hands: her right with the zip ties choking her index, fourth, and pinky. They were black and all puffed up. The nails were lifted at their ends as though they had been smashed with a hammer. On her left hand, Cindy's wedding ring finger was totally gone. An empty space remained where the symbol of lifelong commitment and undying love had been worn for five years. Both hands were swollen in reaction to the disarticulation and digital death seeping into them. And lastly, there were the three photos of her rotting ring finger with Martin's wedding band sewn to it.

"All of her wounds were very neat," Emergency Room physician, Peter Trunkle had testified. "They'd been sutured around the edges to limit blood loss, and Cochran had even used sterile gloves and applied antibiotics. The wounds had also been dressed with sterile bandages. Cindy wasn't going to die from blood loss or infection if Cochran could help it."

Some of the more interesting testimony I read came from the guard who found Cindy. He described hearing noises inside the van, Cindy's ghastly appearance, and the operating room set-up, including all sorts of instruments, drugs and IV bags.

Another medical expert witness was an anesthesiologist—just as Martin had been—Dr. Michael Kovac. He commented on the photographs, Cindy's toxicology screen, and the chemical analysis of the solutions that had been delivered intravenously.

"The photos show a cleverly improvised portable operating room," Kovac testified. "I'm impressed with the lighting system and the infusion configuration. The three high-intensity flashlights attached to the van's ceiling would've provided very good illumination. The IV bags and tubing were arranged so the solution could slowly drip into Cindy's blood stream at a controlled rate, over a couple of days, without needing an electric IV pump. Based on the empty vials found in the van, I believe that Ms. Jenkins probably received around four grams of pentothal and five grams of ketamine during her ordeal. Sodium pentothal is a barbiturate that's commonly used to induce general anesthesia, and ketamine hydrochloride is another anesthetic known to have "dissociative" qualities. In other words, ketamine disconnects the mind and body, so that a person doesn't respond to stimuli in the usual fashion. Ms. Jenkins could've remained perfectly motionless while her face was mutilated, her finger amputated, and an ice pick thrust into her back, severing her spinal cord. These drugs would have rendered her unconscious and unable to resist her attacker."

The court documents also recounted Cindy's medical treatments during the months that it took authorities to capture Martin and bring him to trial. Cindy underwent numerous surgical procedures to graft skin onto her face, chest, and genitals. The zip-tied fingers required amputation. She had to have a colostomy to divert feces away from the chemical burns on her bottom, so it could heal without infection. And she wore a urinary catheter for months. Intensive and extensive physical therapy helped to assist her with her paraplegia, and psychotherapy was utilized to help her cope with the insanity of her situation.

After combing through the evidence, witnessing the appalling photos, and reading what was recorded during Martin's prosecution for abducting and assaulting his former love, my work in Albany was complete.

11

The Rest of the Story

So, now I had interviewed Martin *and* Cindy, her mom, and a college friend. I had reviewed court documents, police reports, and eyewitnesses to Cindy's rescue and mutilated, near-death state. But I still had a few holes to fill in. Of greatest interest was a need to flesh out what the couple had been like prior to their marital difficulties, what their individual characteristics were, and who they were as a couple.

Martin had been quick to point out that Cindy's tryst with Trip was the beginning of their marital discord. He blamed his treatment during the divorce and its outcome as the catalyst for his vengeful rampage. He held Thornton and Cindy responsible for inciting the murderous intent within him. *And* he said that his son's kidnapping and death were the reason that he tortured his former lover.

Cindy did allow that Martin had been the man of her dreams when they first met; but after he found out about her liaison with Trip, her dream partner became her blackest nightmare. Martin had gone crazy. He became a killer, her torturer, and sentenced her to a lifetime of paralysis and pain.

I decided that I might find out more—and hopefully less-biased—opinions by interviewing her close friends from the late eighties and early nineties. I arranged to interview two of her girlfriends from Tacoma.

In a quaint waterfront bar and grill overlooking

Commencement Bay, I met two of Cindy's former girl-friends, Kat McDonald and Adrienne Shipman, when they strolled into the nearly empty bar about twenty minutes after our agreed meeting time. I was sitting at the bar, sipping a Perrier with lime. when the two breezed up to me, took me by the hand and led me out onto the dock. We sat at an umbrella table, in a gentle wind that occasionally mussed Adrienne's long blonde hair. Even though both women were in their forties, they were still quite attractive and youthful. Both had athletic builds, and each wore stylish clothing. The two were in a very good mood, and began chatting as though we were all old friends.

Their first concern was Cindy. When had I last seen her? How did she look? How was she feeling? Could they do anything for her? I began to answer their questions as best I could and gave them some background on my interest in the Cochrans' tale. But before I got too far, Kat interrupted. "Mr. Fontaine, I wish you could have known Cindy back then. She was a beautiful girl—both physically and mentally—I guess that's how you would say it. She was so much fun to be with. In fact, they were *both* a lot of fun—Cindy *and* Martin."

"That's right!" Adrienne agreed. "And Cindy was a good friend, maybe my *best* friend way back then." Then, "Of course, you are now, Kat."

The girls smiled brightly at each other and briefly held hands across the table. It reminded me of the old days—when Kelly and I were more affectionate, sharing tender touches and loving glances. It made my heart smile.

"When we first met, Cindy was deeply in love with Martin," Adrienne continued, "and they did everything

130

together. They ran on the beach for exercise, they went to the gym together — that's where I met Cindy — and they even went sailing and fishing together."

"Oh, and they loved the mountains too!" added Kat. "Remember? They were always going hiking and camping. Martin loved to go backpacking up in the mountains. He especially loved Rainier."

"Yeah, I remember," Adrienne agreed, "and they were always so sweet to each other. I never heard them fuss, or fight. They were always holding hands and hugging and kissing — you know, tastefully."

"So, they sound like perfectly normal people before the affair," I said.

Kat replied, "Yes they were. I was actually kinda jealous. I had a boyfriend back then, and we planned to get married and be as in love as Cindy and Martin, but he turned out to be a jerk. Anyway, we split up even before Cindy did."

"I never did really like old Z-28 Tony," Adrienne confided. "The car was nice, but he didn't treat you as good as he should have. And he was always looking at me kinda funny, like he would like to . . . oh, never mind," said Adrienne, and then her face flushed. She looked like she wished she hadn't said anything.

"You never told me that!" Kat exclaimed.

Adrienne reached out for Kat's hand again, and offered an embarrassed smile. Before the moment was lost, Adrienne's feeble grin turned into a bright beam. We were joined by one of their friends, Raymond, who brought four margaritas to the table. He loosely hugged and air-kissed Kat and Adrienne, and shook my hand weakly as he introduced himself.

After sampling her drink a couple of times, Kat

leaned across the table and said, "I'm sorry for interrupting, Mr. Fontaine. Please go on with your story. Oh, Raymond, Pierre was starting to tell us about actually meeting Doctor Martin Cochran!"

"Yes—in prison! On death row!" chimed in Adrienne.

"Oh, my word!" Raymond blurted out, in an attempted hushed tone, as he covered his mouth with his fist. His eyes bulged and he scooted his chair back a bit. "You were in prison?" he asked, innocently.

"No, no, not in prison for a crime," I replied. "Just to interview Dr. Cochran.,"

"Well, please go on, Mr. Fontaine—do tell!"

"Pierre, please," I interrupted.

"Oh yes, Pierre. I'm fascinated," admitted Raymond. " I've heard so much about the mad doctor, but I never actually met him."

So I retold the story of how I met and interviewed Martin during his last two days on earth, including witnessing his execution on day two. I didn't waste time going into great detail, because I wanted to hear what the two women had to say, rather than listen to myself jabber on and on. When I finished, all three were in awe.

In unison they all responded.

"My word!!" said Raymond.

"Oh! My goodness!" exclaimed Adrienne.

And, with her eyes open the widest, "WOW!" shouted Kat.

They couldn't believe what I'd done. And they surely couldn't fathom my witnessing Martin's death!

After a moment's silence, during which each of the three friends interrogated my eyes for signs of madness, Adrienne quietly asked, "Well Pierre, how did you meet

Cindy? Did Martin tell you where to find her? How could he know?"

"No. Actually she was present at his execution," I replied. " I met her there."

"You've got to be kidding!" responded Adrienne. "Cindy watched him die too?"

"I don't blame her one bit," said Kat. "After what I heard that he did to her, I don't blame her one bit. I would've wanted to stick the poisoned needle in his arm myself if he'd done that to me!"

"Amen, sisters," Raymond chimed. He finished his drink and held up his finger as a signal for us to wait. He went to the bar and came back with more margaritas.

The girls had begun to whisper among themselves, and, when Raymond returned, Kat said, "Okay, now tell us about Cindy."

So I told them about seeing Cindy's name in the register and about the woman wearing the big floppy hat and huge dark glasses sitting in a wheelchair. I told them about how she was crying in the witness room, and how my suspicions were confirmed when I overheard the warden consoling her. And then, I described how I caught up to her in the guard shack, and her unwillingness to be interviewed then, which, of course, I understood. Finally, I told them about the chaplain, the notebooks, and Cindy's outrage when she thought that I was Martin's biographer, who would be writing something about them without her side of the story.

"Cindy called me just a few weeks ago. It'd been about three months since Martin's death. She had reconsidered, and now wanted to talk to me so that I could hear *her* side of the story."

"So what did she say? Can you tell us, or do we

have to wait for the book?" asked Kat.

"Please do tell if you can!" piped Raymond. "Everyone loves a juicy story. And this is one helluva tale!"

"Hey! She was our friend, not some movie actress!" chided Adrienne.

"Sorry. You're right," conceded Raymond. "How insensitive of me."

The tequila was setting in. And I tried to keep my lips from getting too loose. Even so, it took me half a margarita to describe how we met in Springfield, and how pitiful their friend's life had become. Tears puddled the girls' eyes as I retold Cindy's memories of her son being hit by a car and basically dying in her arms. And the tears actually flowed, as I recounted Cindy's recollections of her abduction and torture. Finally, I summarized her sufferings while hospitalized; her multiple surgeries; the ordeals of paralysis and rehab; and all of her miserable, depressing years since surviving the brutal attack. Even Raymond, who had never met Cindy, was close to tears and angry as hell at Martin.

"She is so strong," breathed Adrienne.

"Oh my God! How horrible," whispered Kat.

"God love her," Raymond said, as he reached for his friends' hands and gave them each a loving squeeze.

We all sat in silence for a few moments, and then softly, slowly Adrienne began to tell how she and Cindy met and her recollections of Cindy and Martin.

The two women had met shortly after Cindy married Martin and moved to town. They were close from the beginning, hung out and partied together often. When the marriage went sour, Cindy confided in Adrienne, who was a good listener and a rock in the storm.

Cindy told her about all of the hours that Martin had to spend at work.

"Cindy felt alone and abandoned when Martin had to work late, or had to spend all weekend at the hospital," Adrienne reported. "Did you know that doctors regularly work sixty hours in a row? They go to the hospital on Friday evening and don't come back home until Monday morning. It's insane! And I don't think that it's safe. Anyway, especially during those times Cindy felt deserted and depressed. It *really* got bad after Marcus was born. She had so much to do and no one to help her. I really felt sorry for her and I offered to help — you know — come over and watch the baby while she cleaned, or while she shopped, or something. And I did that a couple of times, but usually she wouldn't let me. I think she didn't want to bother anyone. Well, she got lonelier and lonelier, and more depressed. We talked about it some, and she tried a couple of things like getting together with the girls while a babysitter watched Marcus. But it wasn't until she started to take tennis lessons that she began to snap out of it.

At first, I thought that the regular exercise was the reason for her improved outlook, but soon she confided that it was because of her instructor, Trip. He made her feel young and beautiful and alive when they were together."

Adrienne paused and took a long sip of her margarita. Then, after thoughtful consideration, she continued, "Cindy felt guilty about cheating, but figured that the affair wouldn't last and that soon she'd rededicate her heart to Martin. He really was a prince, she told me — even-tempered, hard-working, a great provider, and a talented lover. I was stunned when Cindy told me about the affair, and I told her to stop seeing Trip immediately. But, of course, she didn't. So, in an effort to be a good friend, I tried to hold my tongue. I tried to just listen."

Apparently, Kat had become part of the inner circle approximately a year before Cindy became pregnant. She told of how she, Cindy, Adrienne, and Cassie Rocotti got together about once a week for afternoon drinks and gossip. Usually they would motor around the bay on Cassie's Cal 39', a gorgeous boat that rode well, offered wonderful privacy and allowed all on board to relax.

"I thought Cindy had a marriage made in heaven," Kat said. "She had a beautiful home, a handsome husband, plenty of money, *and* the time to enjoy it. She was smart and gorgeous and funny. She was a good friend who'd listen to your problems and help if she could. I couldn't believe it when she finally told us about Trip."

Adrienne interrupted, "We'd noticed that things had changed after Marcus was born. You know—lots of women get a little crazy after child birth, but usually they straighten out pretty quick." She took the last sip of her drink and continued. "We even talked to Cindy about it, but as the weeks passed it seemed that she got more and more depressed. She skipped our little weekly get-togethers too many times, and didn't lose the extra baby weight as quickly as she wanted to. Then, one day, a year, or so after Marcus was born, Martin suggested that she take up tennis, get some lessons maybe. Cassie knew a great guy—a tennis coach in fact—who could help Cindy learn. As it turned out, Cassie and her 'great guy', Trip, were already an item."

Now it was Kat's turn again. "Yeah, they were already screwing, but none of us knew it. Cassie had been seeing Trip for about six months. And she kept the se-

136

cret to the bitter end."

"That's right! She never told us. In fact, it was Trip who told Cindy, once they became lovers. And, Cassie dumped him *because* of Cindy," added Adrienne.

The girls played off of each other, one telling part of the story, and the other finishing it. According to them, Cindy occasionally played tennis with Cassie and soon decided to take lessons from Trip. After a while, Cindy and Trip were spending more time together than the tennis pro and Cassie. At about the same time, Cassie's marriage exploded. She hired the most evil divorce lawyer possible. Together, they began a program of irritation, aggravation, and intimidation, aimed at infuriating the soon-to-be EX, and goading him into misbehavior that outweighed Cassie's infidelity.

The plan worked, and, after an ugly war, Callie walked away with the house, the Cal 39', a Lexus, an allowance for domestic help, and a sizable monthly alimony check. When Cindy's indiscretions caught up with her, she retained Cassie's champion: Elizabeth Steele.

Elizabeth Steele, Attorney at Law, was well known as the city's most venomous divorce attorney. And she promptly turned the tables on Dr. Cochran. Martin's complaint of Cindy's infidelity was quickly overshadowed by accusations of physical violence, public reports of a restraining order violation, and innuendos of professional misconduct, *including* narcotic diversion and deviant behavior with patients while they were asleep. Martin Cochran's character and integrity became the court's focus, even though none of the accusations were substantiated. Cindy's defender succeeded in destroying Martin's reputation, and publicly humiliated him.

Adrienne believed that Martin went crazy because of the stress that he endured while fighting Ms. Steele's terrorist tactics.

"Martin had always seemed so sweet," Adrienne said. "I just couldn't believe it when I heard that he was suspected of murdering that private eye. And then, when Cindy's story broke, I was in shock, but I could see how he could've gone nuts after what he went through during the divorce. You know, Cindy cheating on him, losing his job, his house, his reputation, his precious child—and all of *the horrible* publicity."

"Yeah, but that doesn't excuse him for what he did to Cindy and the P.I.," replied Kat.

"I know, I know, but a bunch of it just wasn't true—Cindy even said so," countered Adrienne.

"Well," Raymond quickly added, before anyone else could speak again, "as you girls know, I myself have been on the receiving end of Ms. Elizabeth Steele's evil schemes."

Raymond's story mirrored that of Martin and Mr. Rocotti. Ms. Steele had done her best to make Raymond's life miserable. It was as though she had a list of dirty tricks that she used, in order to redirect the court's attention away from real issues surrounding the couple's breakup. Raymond wound up surrendering in anger and frustration. Though they were together for only five years, Edward was awarded half of the value of Raymond's lucrative art importing business, his North Slope historic home, and the 1977 Porsche 911.

During our lengthy conversation, the girls reminisced about the good times with Cindy and Martin. They told of parties that they had all attended, and an incredible sailing adventure with the Cochrans. By all accounts, Martin and Cindy were normal, happy people prior to Marcus' birth. Then Cindy became somewhat depressed, but there was still no reason to predict their breakup. According to her friends, even during the affair with Trip, Cindy wasn't planning to leave Martin. In fact, she planned to rededicate herself to her husband.

Before she left for Albany, the two didn't know about the liaison with Thornton. Cindy had never let them in on that secret. They only knew that things had gotten out of hand when Martin became irate one night. There was a huge argument, and Cindy left the house with Marcus about midnight. They said that argument signaled the real end of the marriage.

Adrienne remembered the night that Cindy left town. "Cindy was already freaking out because Trip had disappeared, and her lawyer was almost killed in a terrible car wreck. Anyway, I had just gotten home from the gym when the phone rang. It was Cindy, and she was hysterical! She said she'd just heard on the news the story of Martin's private eye being murdered in South Carolina, and that Martin was the prime suspect. The FBI and everybody was looking for him. Cindy was crying and really scared. I asked her why Martin would kill the P.I., and why would he have been in South Carolina? And why was she so freaked? Did she think that Martin was going to come and kill *her*?

"She said she was leaving Tacoma immediately. Martin scared her to death, and she was afraid he was going to kill her and take Marcus somewhere, probably Canada or Mexico. She told me about the private eye threatening her and basically forcing her to have sex with him twice—and that Martin found out. That's why he murdered Thornton.

"I couldn't believe it! Cindy had sex with that P.I. too! No wonder Martin went crazy. I probably would have too. Anyway, she just wanted me to know she was leaving, and that she didn't know where she'd end up. I asked if she might go to her mom's, but she said definitely not. She was too afraid that Martin would find her there. She was in a huge hurry and couldn't talk but for just a minute, and wanted me to know what was happening. And to let her friends know, and to thank them for being good friends.

We probably talked for about two minutes. She was crying the whole time. Then, I didn't hear from her for about a month."

Kat broke in. "Yeah, she called me a few weeks after she had left town, but she wouldn't tell anybody where she was . . . so Martin couldn't find out. She was still pretty scared but had started to settle down some, according to her. She said that she was going to try to get a job, and put the past behind her. She told me that she was truly sorry things had turned out the way they had. I told her that I missed her, that I loved her, and hoped we'd see each other again someday."

Tears came to Kat's eyes when she finished her story. "I never heard from her again. The next thing I heard was that Marcus had been hit by a car, and Martin had almost killed Cindy. Even after all these years, Cindy has never called me. I guess that she was just too busy healing and staying alive to worry about her old life and friends."

Adrienne finished the tragedy. "Well, Cindy did call *me*. Twice, in fact. The first time was about a month after she left Tacoma. She let me know she was okay. She asked about her friends in town, and if I had heard any-

thing about Martin. All I knew was that he was suspected of the private eye's murder, and was maybe hiding
out in Canada, according to the news.

"Then she called me a couple of days after Marcus
had died. She was nearly going crazy! She was blaming
herself and was in so much pain. She couldn't stop crying. I offered to help in any way that I could — even to
go to where ever she was and be with her — but she
didn't want that. I felt helpless, and so I just cried with
her. And I told her I loved her over and over again. It
was truly pitiful, Pierre. The next thing I remember is
that Martin had found her and tortured her in Trip's van,
and left her for dead. I called her mom, but she was way
too busy to talk. God, that's been so long ago, and it
seems like just yesterday. What a horrible story! Do you
think we should call her now, after all these years, Mr.
Fontaine?"

I didn't know. And I felt bad for bringing up all
those painful memories. But I was glad that I made the
trip to Tacoma. Cindy's old friends allowed me to get a
more rounded picture of Martin and his former wife.
Additionally, Raymond's dealings with Ms. Steele
helped me to more fully understand how stressful the
divorce had been. And finally, maybe most importantly,
Adrienne and Kat remembered a couple of Martin's
buddies' names.

The next morning, I drove up to Poverty Bay. What
a misnomer! The houses there where huge — many of
them had tennis courts. The ones on the bay had walk-
ways, or driveways, down to boathouses and waterfront
cottages. Mercedes and Jaguars were common, and I
even saw one Lamborghini parked outside of a mansion

with a five-car garage.

I found that Ted Wright, MD, had retired early — just a couple of years ago — and had moved to some exotic South Pacific island. His ex-wife, Bunny, who still used his last name and still lived in the home that they'd shared, graciously let me in and answered my questions as best she could. She had only met Martin two, maybe three times, before she and Ted divorced. She remembered him as handsome and strong. He had good manners and nice teeth. She said that Ted and Martin must've become buddies later, because, while she was married to Ted, the two men were just business partners in the anesthesia group.

She was shocked by the public accusations leveled against Dr. Cochran during his divorce, and even more stunned when Martin was named as a suspect in Thornton's murder. She'd followed Cindy and Martin's story while it had been a headline, but hadn't heard anything new for years, until the recent coverage of Martin's execution.

"It's almost inconceivable, Mr. Fontaine, that a man of his education would stoop so low as to murder someone, and then, torture his wife!" She sat forward in her chair and studied my eyes as though determining if I were on his side or hers.

I had to agree with Ms. Wright — *and* I told her so.

"He must've really enjoyed sailing, if he spent much time with Ted, because Ted was forever traipsing off on some grand sailing adventure. He loved to cruise the Passage. He loved the scenery, the danger — all the little islands and rocks that you simply *must* avoid. And he loved to brag about having sailed to Alaska — *alone* — probably more than anyone else alive."

While standing on the threshold of Bunny's marble entryway, I thanked her for her time and hospitality. She warmly shook my hand, smiled brightly, and quickly added, "Oh! I just had a thought, Mr. Fontaine. Ted was also good friends with Jacob Moore. He is also an anesthesiologist and a sailor, and I know that at least once, Ted, Jacob, and Dr. Cochran went sailing together. Perhaps Dr. Moore would have something to add to your story."

"Thanks," I said, as I departed. "I'll check into it. Thanks so much."

Then, I drove through the mid morning traffic until I found Pacific Highway South. Once there, it only took a few minutes to arrive at 348th, and then head west toward Brown's Point in search of another of Martin's friends.

Victor Carr was the other name that the girls remembered. According to Adrienne, Mr. Carr had been Martin's best buddy. Adrienne remembered "Vic" from parties she'd attended at the Cochrans'. She recalled that the former Army Ranger would often regale them with one of his many big adventures. And that he and Martin would always try to trump each other's story.

Carr lived on a Westsail 32', in a slip close to Brown's Point. His name was not in the phone book, and I probably would have never found him if Adrienne hadn't pointed across the bay to the marina where he had a slip.

He wasn't home, so I left a note on the cabin door and another one with the marina's manager. Then, I went back to my hotel room and looked up Dr. Jacob Moore's phone number and address.

Dr. Moore wasn't at home, but his wife was. She remembered Martin, but was in a hurry and didn't have time to answer my questions.

"You can try his cell," she said, "but he probably won't answer. He's got a couple of big cases today."

I took a chance and dialed the number. He answered on the second ring, and sounded rushed. I froze for a second, then told a little white lie: "Dr. Moore? I'm very sorry to bother you. I'm certain that you're in a huge hurry, but Martin Cochran wanted me to tell you hello and to say thanks for your friendship."

"What!? Martin Cochran? Who is this?" the doctor almost shouted, with a tone of disbelief in his voice.

"My name is Pierre Fontaine. I spoke with Martin just before he died. He said if I was ever in Tacoma I should look you up and give you that message. I'm really sorry if I've interrupted—"

"No, no, no. That's alright. I'm just between cases. I'm setting up for a craniotomy. But thanks for the message, Mister . . ."

"Fontaine. Pierre Fontaine. I'm a writer. I interviewed Martin on death row, and witnessed his execution."

"What? You've got to be kidding me! You watched Martin die? Be put to death?"

"Yes sir, I did." And I felt the tide of the conversation turn in my favor.

"And he wanted you to tell me hello and thanks?"

"Yes, Dr. Moore he did," I said, crossing my fingers to ward off the bad karma that comes with telling lies.

Dr. Moore's twelve-hour shift ended at 7:30 p.m.,

and we met at eight in a local dive next to Capt'n Pat's Marina on Titlow beach. The beginning of the conversation was almost a carbon copy of yesterday's with Adrienne and Kat. I explained how I became interested in Martin Cochran's sad tale, and of my interactions with both Cindy and him. Dr. Moore listened patiently and grazed on fish and chips, washed down with an "Oly."

"It's really hard to believe, you know, this whole story. Martin was one of the nicest guys you'd ever want to meet . . . .and he was a damn good doctor, one of our best back then." He finished the beer and thought for a second. "Martin and I were pretty good friends. We shared a lot of interests and we practiced medicine similarly."

I munched on my deep-fried, beer-battered Halibut sandwich and curly fries, while Dr. Moore continued.

"You probably don't know that there are about a hundred ways of administering anesthesia. Well maybe not quite so many, but Martin and I used pretty much the same techniques, and we always had really good results. You know, patients are given surveys and they always rated Martin very high." Moore ordered us both new beers and stated, "That's why it was so shocking for us to hear those crazy allegations of misconduct and drug diversions."

"Yeah. I've been wondering about that," I said. "Do ya think all that stuff was just a nasty tactic—"

"In fact, I actually do. I think Cindy's lawyer concocted those stories just to hurt Martin and to distract the Court's attention away from Cindy's affair. Ya know, once, Martin told me that during one of their first court appearances, his attorney presented some of the photos the private eye had taken. The judge looked at 'em and

145

asked Cindy's attorney for an explanation. She didn't comment on the pictures. Martin said she totally ignored them, and, instead, told the judge that 'they' were looking into some accusations of Martin diverting anesthesia drugs and molesting women while they were asleep in the O.R. I just couldn't believe it. Martin was livid and understandably scared. He said the hardest thing he'd ever done was to <u>not</u> kill the lying bitch right there. And I don't blame him for being furious."

After a few beats, Moore continued. "Well, maybe you don't know — but no one *ever* came forward to point a finger and substantiate the claims. But the group finally had to let him go. It was the wrong thing to do, but there was so much bad publicity that the hospital pressured our chief into firing Martin. It was total bullshit!"

I shook my head and sipped on the beer. The doctor sipped his, and we watched the waitress go by. He hadn't blinked for what seemed like minutes, as he sat silent, pensive. He rubbed his chin and, finally, wearily closed his eyes as he turned to me and asked, "Can you tell me something?"

I held my breath.

"How did my friend die?"

The question hit me squarely in the gut, and I squirmed a bit. Softly and respectfully, I recounted Martin's final moments on Earth. When I had finished, my hands had grown cold, and a light sweat rode my forehead and trickled down my back. Martin's good friend sat silent. His eyes had drifted away from being locked onto mine, as I recited Martin's last words, told how he had laid back on the gurney and peacefully awaited death. Jacob Moore's eyes filled with little pools of tears. He dipped his chin and slowly nodded his head. I could feel his pain and loss. He had the look of resigned acceptance. He understood what Martin certainly would have known way back when: that Cochran's vengeful deeds would place him on an inexorable course leading to his own death. And, that in Martin's mind, the trade was worth it.

Sadness gripped Moore for a moment. In a second, he sat up straight and asked, "What more can I tell you, Pierre? That Martin was a great guy? That he was a good friend, and, as far as I know, a good husband before the divorce? That he was a good father? Well he was all of those things and more. I really don't think that he would've ever harmed anyone without all the harassment and lies. I don't believe that he misbehaved at work. But I *do* think that something deep inside snapped. His brain malfunctioned. The killer that you saw on death row was not the guy that I was buddies with."

There was an uncomfortably long silence while Dr. Moore searched my eyes. Then, he checked his watch, said it was getting late, stood, and shook my hand. He pitched fifty bucks on the table, started to say something, turned, and walked away. As he passed the waitress he said, "That should take care of it."

I sat dumbstruck for a minute, my stomach queasy. Pangs of guilt rumbled around in my unsettled midsection. Once again I had uncorked old memories and salted old wounds.

I returned to my room and had a restless night.

The next afternoon, I paid Victor Carr a second visit and found him unloading and drying out camping gear all over the deck and the dock. He looked like an adventurer: shaggy, salt and pepper hair that hadn't seen a comb in forever; a week's worth of nappy beard; a sun tanned, weather-creased face with brilliant azure eyes, and a pirate's smile.

He shook my extended hand and politely listened to my introduction, and, as he let my words soak in, he continued to fuss with his gear. In a minute, he turned to me with suspicion pinching his face, and inspected me.

"Mr. Fontaine, how did you know that I was one of Martin's friends? Did he tell you? And how in the world did ya find me?"

"Call me Pierre, please and, well, no. I'm afraid that Martin didn't mention your name. Sorry. Actually, one of Cindy's friends gave me your name."

"You talked with Cindy?"

"I did . . ."

"My God, how is she? I never had the nerve to call or visit after—"

"She's alive and okay I guess, but in pitiful shape— paralyzed and disfigured." And then I briefly described our interactions and Cindy's mention of her girlfriends.

"Adrienne Shipman gave me your name. I met her and Kat McDonald yesterday in that little tavern across the bay . . . Katie Downs. Cool place. Anyway, she pointed out this marina. So I just got lucky."

"Huh!" Carr exclaimed. "I haven't seen those girls in quite some time . Still good lookin' I bet."

"Yep," I replied.

After some thought, Vic invited me onboard, offered me a seat and a beer. He wanted to hear as much about Martin as I could recall. So I went into some detail, telling him about my journey thus far. When I finished my story and my beer, we sat in silence for a few moments. He shook his head in disbelief.

"That is totally incredible! That is the wildest story I've ever heard! You actually wormed your way onto death row and talked with Martin? And he invited you to his execution? And then you watched him be put to death? Freakin' insane!"

He took the last slug of his beer, studied the heavens in amazement, shook his head even more, and said, "Whew! Man maybe Martin was nuts, but I think that maybe *you're* nuts too!"

The gulls squawked. Vic studied the sky and the waters. I studied his face. Would he talk to me about Martin? Would he tell me about their friendship? Would he help me understand who Martin was before his break with sanity?

"Whatcha gonna do?" he asked. "Write a book about Martin and Cindy?"

"Maybe . . . I guess so. I'm really not sure just yet."

He rolled up his tent, bullied it into a nylon stuff sack, turned and said, "We were good friends, Pierre. I loved him like a brother. We had lots in common and we did a lot of cool stuff together. He was an honorable man—did all the right things. He served his country; he put his life on the line. He saved other soldiers' lives. He went to school and got a great job, busted his ass for his family. He lived the American Dream. He was a great guy! You shoulda known him back then. I'm really sorry things turned out the way they did," Carr said sadly. He shook his head slowly back and forth, as he inspected the deck, deep in thought.

Vic told of how he and Martin met while each was hiking around Mount Rainier. "It'd been raining like hell for two days. I was as cold and miserable as I've ever been. I'd been out for a week, and had planned to be home the day before, but the rain had washed away the little log bridges across several creeks. I had to scout out other crossings, and that took a huge amount of time. I probably burned ten hours trying to find places to cross—and I even took a swim! The current was so strong in this one creek that it knocked me down. I damn near drowned! My pack was like an anchor. It was already ten pounds heavier with everything in it already soaked. It pulled me down and dragged me downstream with the current. I must have gone a quarter mile before I could get my footing and get out—just before this huge sweeper would've snagged me and probably killed me.

"Anyway, after I got out, I got back on the trail and walked about a mile or so till I came to a little shelter made out of pine boughs and a couple of tarps. There was a little fire going, and I called out, 'Hello to whoever's in the tent!' Martin popped his head out and was all smiles from ear to ear. He invited me under the tarps, and, in short order, gave me a hot cup of green tea and honey. It was the best drink that I ever had. He'd been hunkered down since that morning and had dried out most of his clothes and gear. By the time I finished the tea and my soggy Slim Jim, the rain had stopped. Martin very graciously loaned me a dry shirt and a jacket. I put up my tent under the trees, close to the fire.

"We spent the evening drying my stuff and telling stories about our military days along with some other crazy adventures. We really hit it off. Then, we hiked out together the next day, again in the pouring rain. The wildest thing was, when we got to the trailhead, there were a couple of forest rangers and a rescue party heading in to try to find a father and daughter who hadn't shown up on time. They were two days overdue according to the wife.

"Martin didn't hesitate. Even though it was pouring and he was tired and hungry, he immediately volunteered to help the search party. He was supposed to be back at the hospital for a twenty-four-hour shift in a couple of days, but he told the rangers that he'd help if they could radio someone who could call his wife to tell her why he was late. They did. He turned right around and followed them back into the bush. I felt terrible. I didn't go with them, because I *absolutely* had to get back. I was overdue myself and would lose my job if I didn't show up the next day."

"Wow," I said.

"Yeah, that was the kind of man Martin was. He had a heart of gold and was always ready to help anyone. They found the dad and kid—saved their lives probably. They were lost and hypothermic. Martin wrapped the girl in his sleeping bag and carried her out. He said it was about five miles. Ha! Have you ever carried a waterlogged pack and an eleven year old for five miles, Pierre? Me neither—and I doubt I could. Plus it was probably more like *ten* miles!"

Carr got us each another beer. "You wanna to know who Martin really was, Pierre?" he continued. "I hope you've got a couple of days, then maybe I'll be able to tell you about half of the story."

I smiled and continued listening. He told of meeting Cindy and being a part of the couple's early life, before parenthood. He remembered Marcus' birth and being at some of the parties thrown in the child's honor—a baby shower, birthdays, and such. Vic and Martin were best friends.

"He didn't tell me about the marriage difficulties for a long time," Carr went on. "Then one day he said that he suspected Cindy of having an affair, and how he'd hired a private eye to keep tabs on her. I was floored! I knew Cindy wasn't her normal perky self, but I would never have guessed what was really going on. Martin was angry and embarrassed, but he told me about Cindy's 'private tennis lessons' — showed me some photos of the tennis pro and his wife sneaking into a cheap motel. We talked about what he should do. He wanted her to be happy, and didn't really want to break up, but he couldn't get over the thought of some other man's hands all over his wife. He thought if he confronted her they could talk things over, maybe work things out, but it didn't go down like that. Well, you know."

According to Carr, Martin's demeanor changed after the confrontation and argument about the affair. Martin seemed to be resigned — the marriage was doomed.

"As the weeks went by the situation became more noxious," said Carr. "Martin became more depressed and angry. He started talking more about Vietnam and the battles he fought, the enemies he'd killed. Sometimes he would say, 'boy war is so nice — it's simple — you're pissed off with somebody so, ya just kill 'em. No talking, no arguing, no lawyers, or courts, or arbitration. You just fuckin' kill 'em, Vic.'"

Vic said that he and Martin met often during the first few months of the separation. They'd have a few beers and try to laugh, but Martin was slowly becoming more involved with the divorce process, sucked into a black hole of pain, anger, and self doubt. Finally, Martin didn't feel like doing very much. He told Vic he felt trapped, and was tired of being bullied by Cindy's lawyer. The courts were not trying to flesh out who was right or wrong, or make decisions based on moral correctness. They seemed to be punishing him in response to sensational allegations made by Ms. Steele.

"You wouldn't believe it, Pierre! The crap that that evil bitch lawyer came up with was unreal. She actually stood up in court and accused Martin of molesting women while they were under anesthesia! And she said he was probably using narcotics, or selling them, or something. Can you imagine that?" Vic's eyes were wild with anger.

"Martin was a respected doctor," he continued. "Hell, he was a Purple Heart hero! He was even captured—a POW. That damned lawyer just threw out all these accusations—never proved a one of 'em. The newspaper printed the crap; it turned into a huge media circus. The hospital wasn't happy and asked him to leave. It was all total bullshit!"

Vic's second beer was drained, and he became more animated by the minute. I think if Ms. Steele had walked by just then she would have been in mortal danger.

"When the divorce was finalized and the custody rights were announced, Martin came unglued. He'd already been forced out of his home and fired from his job. Now, the judge ordered him to pay child support and alimony to the tune of seven thousand dollars a month until Marcus was nineteen. Also, he gave Cindy sole custody. Martin was only allowed supervised visitation twice a month for three hours, every other Sunday, and a phone call to Marcus on the other Sundays at 7:00 p.m.

"Martin was livid, Pierre, and he had every right to be. The night that he told me all of this, I could sense that things had changed. He was enraged. Pure hell was in his eyes. He was living in a tiny apartment downtown with nothing—no family, no job. He'd lost all hope of being the father that he wanted to be. His life had become meaningless. He didn't know how he'd ever pay the money, and, because of all of the bad publicity, he probably couldn't ever get another job. He also told me about Cindy and Thornton's screwing around. I couldn't believe it! Cindy screwing *two* guys! I almost fell over. Martin was a good man. He didn't deserve all this shit. I woulda snapped too."

"Wow," I said, "that really sucks. He didn't go into all that detail and he didn't tell me about being wounded or captured in the war. His captain said Cochran had been hit by a grenade, but *nothing* about being a POW."

"Yeah well, Martin didn't like to talk about it, but he was captured and held prisoner for a couple of days. He was beaten up. They even cut off his left ear and his left pinky finger. You didn't see that, I guess?"

"No, I didn't."

"It's a long story," Vic continued, "but suffice it to say that during a patrol, Martin and three other guys came under fire. Two guys were hit and died right there. Martin and the other marine were captured. The gooks took 'em back to their camp and tried to get 'em to talk, and that's when they got his ear and finger. Martin said it was hell, but he didn't give in. The yellow bastards even forced him up a limbless tree and drove *punji* sticks into the ground all around the tree so that if he fell he'd be impaled. He spent the night in that tree holding on for dear life. In the early morning, the flyboys started dropping bombs, and the gooks bugged out, leaving him in the tree. About an hour later, just before he was about to lose his grip, some of our guys moved through the area, found him, and got him down."

"Wow! That's totally incredible," I said, and I wondered what role that experience played in Cindy's torture.

Vic handed me a third beer, which I really didn't want. He opened one for himself, began a new sentence, but then stopped. He collected all of his gear from the dock, tossed it into a couple of plastic bins, and stowed them below. He returned with an old photo album, which he passed to me. Then, with the new beer in hand and the sun about to set, he began telling me about the last time he saw Martin. I thumbed through the pages as he spoke.

"The last time that I saw Martin, it was — oh — maybe a week after the divorce was final," Victor Hugo Carr said, in a quiet, pained voice, with a distant look in his eyes, "he looked like hell. He looked like he had been sleeping in a dumpster — hadn't shaved in days and wearing dirty fatigues. I knew that the last time he had worn camo was in 'nam. I had a sick feeling when he told me that I'd probably never see him again. He never said exactly what was going to happen, but I kinda guessed that Cindy and company were in big trouble. He snapped, Pierre. Martin had had enough and was going to deal out some retribution, spread some misery around — Marine Corps style. I tried to contact Cindy, but never could — even drove to her house, but she was never home."

He took the album, turned to a page near the end, and showed me the last photo taken of Martin and him.

They were smiling, both were suntanned, and Vic was holding Martin's precious child, Marcus.

"We had a couple of beers and talked about some of the old times, and he thanked me for being a good friend, for 'being there.' His eyes filled with tears when he said that. Mine too. He blinked his away then, hit me on the shoulder. He reminded me of the time we had crossed paths with a sow and her cubs just outside of a little log cabin I built way back in the woods. He asked me to always keep that little cabin—just in case of emergencies. Said it'd be good to keep it stocked with some decent beer, some water, and maybe a little food—just in case I ever fell on hard times. Well, I never saw him after that night, Pierre, but sometimes, for about four months, when I would go check on my little hide-out in the weeds, it was obvious that someone had been there. Sometimes all of the supplies would be gone, sometimes not, but it was always cleaned up. Neat as a pin."

Thumbing through the album, I saw that it contained mostly photos of Carr and places that he had been, but several of them included Martin. There were also a few that recorded happy scenes of Martin and Cindy alone, and some of them with Marcus. There was even one with Vic bouncing Marcus on his knee during Marcus' first birthday party. These would have been the pictures that Marcus would have referred to had he lived beyond the messy divorce and its aftermath. They would have proven his parents' happiness, their normalcy. They would have reinforced his feelings of belonging, and refuted the notion of his parents' insanity.

Carr went on to tell me about "some suspicious shit that went down" just after his final meeting with Martin.

He couldn't remember exactly how it all happened, but he did remember that Ms. Steele had a bad car wreck and Trip went missing. About the same time, there came reports of Thornton's murder and Martin's possible involvement.

"When I heard about the private eye's murder, I knew that Martin was probably responsible for the lawyer's wreck *and* Trip's disappearance too. I tried to get in touch with Cindy a couple of times—maybe a week or so before the P.I.'s murder—but she had changed her number and it was unlisted. I didn't want to believe that Martin would have gone so crazy, but I *did* want to warn Cindy that she could be in danger. Well, I never got a hold of her, and I guess that she figured it out anyway and left town.

"I found out about Cindy's attack from my girlfriend at the time. I was in Anguilla, about to weigh anchor and set off across the Atlantic. When I called Trish, she told me that CNN had just carried the story of the crazy assault on Cindy—*and* that Martin did it. I about fell off my chair! I couldn't believe it! I'm tellin' ya, Pierre, Martin had to have gone crazy for real, 'cause the Martin I knew would have never done what he did. I mean, I really believe that he went insane!"

I asked Vic if he had come to Martin's defense in court.

"No, like I said, I was on my trip around the world, and didn't get back to the States 'til it was all over. I was gone twenty-eight months, four days, six hours, and fifteen minutes. So, I missed all the trials and everything. I'm truly sorry that I couldn't say good things about the Martin I had known." Here Vic got a little choked up and his eyes pooled with water.

"I never saw or heard from Martin since that last night when he was in 'cammies,' and he looked like hell. Like I said, he may have been hiding out somewhere around my cabin, but I never saw him. You know, through the years, I've thought about it a lot. Martin never called or sent me a letter. We were like brothers. But I guess if you're crazy you just don't do the things that you normally would've done. Maybe he didn't want to bother me, or maybe he was ashamed. I don't know, but I really did figure he'd get in touch."

Vic finished that sentence and turned away. I could feel his disappointment and pain. I sat in silence for a minute and then asked about his sailing adventure around the world. He took his time, and I was glad, because I needed to chill for a while—until my beer level dropped a bit.

The next day, I dug around in the archives of Tacoma's newspaper and TV station. I already knew most of the story; the news coverage simply added validity to what I'd already been told. But there was some new and interesting information presented.

First, I looked up Thomas Thornton's murder. On August 3, 1995, the *Tacoma Times* shouted this headline on its front page: **"Tacoma PI Murdered, Doctor # 1 Suspect!"** The news article reported that, on the previous day, Thomas Thornton had been found dead hanging in an oak tree at a Columbia, South Carolina golf course and that Tacoma anesthesiologist Dr. Martin Cochran's tennis racquet was found around the victim's neck. It went on to describe the murder scene and the relationship of the deceased to the doctor. It surmised that the killing was connected to the doctor's recent divorce, and reprinted excerpts of former articles relevant to the breakup. The reporter attempted to contact the suspect's ex-wife, but was unsuccessful.

The next day, August 4th, Cindy called Adrienne to inform her that she was leaving town. She loaded up the car, buckled Marcus in, and made a hasty escape.

Two weeks before Cindy fled Tacoma, she read a report that said: "Local attorney, Elizabeth Steele has been involved in a serious accident while driving on I-5. Approximately one hundred yards west of the Pacific Avenue intersection, Ms. Steele's Volvo careened over the center median, swerved across the westbound lanes and came to rest, upside down in a grassy ditch. It took rescue crews an hour and a half to extricate the unconscious attorney. She was rushed to St. Joseph's Medical Center where she is being treated for major burns and other life threatening injuries."

Printed on the same day as Thornton's murder exposé, a follow-up report said the investigation into Ms. Steele's accident found that her car had been fitted with a bomb, which had detonated while she was driving to work. The accident was being treated as an attempted homicide. The article also pointed out that Ms. Steele had been handling the high profile, volatile divorce proceedings of Mrs. Marlaina Conti, the wife of locally infamous businessman Louis Conti, a known associate of imprisoned mobster John Carbone.

I researched the Conti divorce and found it had captured multiple headlines. There was a small empire at stake. At the same time, Mr. Conti was under investigation for a number of shady business dealings — some related to suspected Mafia activities.

An earlier piece, written in mid-July, offered a remarkable statement of Conti's. As he exited the courthouse, reporter Jacqueline Ho asked how the proceedings were going, and Conti replied, "Good afternoon, Jacqueline. What marvelous weather. Don't you think? Yes, well negotiations with my wife are progressing. And her attorney is truly remarkable. I look forward to the day when the venomous Ms. Steele reflects on her incendiary tactics, her acid demeanor, and libelous claims. One day, she may regret her roughshod treatment of respectable citizens. Perhaps her insight will strangle her hubris, humble the exalted 'Queen of the Courts,' and lead her to beg forgiveness from those she's unjustly accused and verbally castrated. Good day, Jacqueline."

I raised my eyebrows at the string of fancy words, which amounted to a thinly veiled threat. It wasn't a long stretch to imagine Conti perpetrating an attempt on Steele's life.

Though Martin's divorce was finalized and had captured some public attention, he was not mentioned as a suspect, yet. But, some of the passages in his notebooks indicate that he was probably responsible for Elizabeth Steele's injuries.

Before interviewing Adrienne, Kat, and Raymond, I didn't know much about Ms. Steele. Cindy had only used her first name, Liz. And so, when I read certain passages in Martin's notes, I had no clue there might have been a connection between the phrases and a crime. I passed it off as a lunatic's ravings — just another one of his poems — but it was probably an indication of Martin's involvement. He wrote:

"steel doors, steel bars,
steel shanks, steel nerves
steely eyes, steele lies

steele flies, steele cries
fire and broken bones
steel jaws of life
steele can be bent
steele can be broken"

And she was broken — forever.

Before I left Tacoma, I spoke with Liz's former secretary. I found that Elizabeth Steele, Attorney at Law, survived her broken bones and burns, but her brain took a major hit. She never returned to her law practice. Instead, she spent the rest of her life in hospitals and, finally, in a nursing home where she died of complications associated with aspiration pneumonia, a result of her brain injury and the inability to swallow correctly. Had Martin killed a lawyer too?

Trip Johnson's disappearance was covered a few times by the media, but was apparently never solved. After Trip didn't show up at work for a couple of days, his employer called his parents. They hadn't heard from him either, but it wasn't uncommon for him to neglect phoning or visiting them for weeks at a time. The Johnsons notified the police after they went to Trip's bungalow and found no sign of him, but definite signs of a struggle — including blood stains on the floor and wall. The police searched for weeks and found nothing — no witnesses, no trail, no Chevy van.

The van showed up in Albany, New York, five months after the tennis pro's disappearance. Martin, the fiend, had taken Trip's mobile love palace and had used it as Cindy's torture chamber. When the Tacoma authorities discovered where the van was and what had happened in it, Martin became the prime suspect in Trip's suspected murder.

As I read the coverage of Trip's case, my memory flashed on the pages of two newspapers found in the van after Cindy's rescue, and I remembered some of Martin's other entries in his books. One of the news pages contained a small article that covered the Forest Service's intention to set ablaze certain slash piles located in the national forest close to Tacoma. The other contained a small article about Ms. Steele's automobile accident. Neither were blatant confessions, but, in retrospect, both were obvious clues to Martin's involvement.

Also, I recalled that he'd written a three-page story about the forest. Buried in the text was a short passage that I now believed was devoted to Trip Johnson. When I got home, I reviewed it:

". . . TRIP, a Path, winding and narrow, mostly hidden from view. No one should see it, it will forever remain a secret, sacred, sublime. Trips can be funny, they may begin innocent, sensuous, splendid, inexorably drawing one in, Nirvana. Then turning, scratching and biting. Pulling you down. Thorns and Poison! The forest is heaven, the forest is hell. Leap for joy at the solitude, the secrecy. Weep in pain for their murder, the slash piles that scar Mother Earth and stain Father Sky. And muffle the cries. A grand place to hide, a lonely place to die. No Trace. No Trace. It's a motto. It's a rule. A no trace trip will never divulge the secret, never emerge with a tale. Yet a tale was told and THE TRIP ENDED in smoke and flame. It wasn't pretty to watch but I did. The bulldozers backed off and the diesel was lit. Black death belched from the slash pile. The flames were not impressive. It smoldered for more than a week. Only grey ash remains."

Was this a description of how Trip died? Burned in

a slash pile in the Great Northwest Woods? Did Martin kill the tennis pro, his ex-wife's lover? Were these obtuse phrases Martin's confession to Trip's murder? Was the poem about bombing Ms. Steele? Had Martin been on a killing spree? Were these the other missions Martin wished he'd time to tell me about?

My god, I thought, *Martin's a murder machine.*

Continuing to investigate, I found that on September 26, 1995 — two days after the event — the *Tacoma Times* carried a front page story of Marcus' tragic death. The headline read: "**Four Year Old Killed In Albany.**" The article explained that Marcus Cochran, four years old, the son of Dr. Martin Cochran and his former wife, Cindy, was killed on September 24, 1995 in Albany, NY, when he ran into the street chasing a ball. Unfortunately, Mrs. Emma White, 78, couldn't stop in time. The child was struck by the automobile, and rushed to Albany Medical Center, where he was pronounced dead. The article added that the boy's father, Dr. Martin Cochran, a former Tacoma area anesthesiologist, was currently wanted by the FBI in connection with the murder of Thomas Thornton, a former area private investigator. Also, that Cochran was a suspect in the disappearance of his ex-wife's former boyfriend, Trip Johnson, who hadn't been seen for two months. And lastly, Dr. Cochran was also a suspect in the explosive auto accident involving Elizabeth Steele, his ex-wife's divorce attorney.

The report of Marcus' tragic death tied together all of the major players in Martin's savage revenge scheme. And, if Martin read the article, he would know where to find Cindy.

Cindy's turn was next. I can't say for certain how

Martin found her, but he did and he carried revenge to depths I could never have imagined prior to hearing Cindy's story. The *Tacoma Times* story began, "On December 14, Ms. Cindy Jenkins—the former Mrs. Martin Cochran—was found nearly dead in Albany, NY. She'd been tied down in the back of a Chevy van owned by her missing boyfriend, Trip Johnson, of Tacoma. The van had been parked in the St. Peter's Hospital parking lot for at least two days with Ms. Jenkins inside." The article described her condition, and said she'd been rushed into the Emergency Department, stabilized, and sent to the ICU for further treatment.

It went on to say, "Ms. Jenkins' former husband, Dr. Martin Cochran, is the prime suspect in this case and others: the disappearance of Trip Johnson; the murder of Thomas Thornton, a private eye, and former employee of Cochran; and the bombing of Elizabeth Steele's automobile. Ms. Steele had been Ms. Jenkins' divorce attorney."

And, five and a half months later, Martin's dastardly saga captured national attention and local headlines again: **"MURDER SUSPECT DR. COCHRAN CAPTURED!!"**

For three consecutive days and a couple more in the following weeks, the *Tacoma Times* and the ABC affiliate, channel 4 KOMO, explored Martin's crimes. They began by retelling the story of Thornton's grisly murder, reminding viewers that Martin had employed the PI during his messy divorce and the evidence of Martin's guilt. Then they detailed Cindy's gruesome assault, describing in nauseating detail Cindy's injuries and an update on her progress back to health. They tied in Trip's disappearance and Ms. Steele's accident, now dubbed "attempted murder."

Most interesting to me was how Martin was captured. On May 7, 1996, some sixty miles from Tacoma near Morton, Washington, a scraggly haired, hobo-bearded, middle-aged bum was seen sorting through the dumpsters behind the hospital. The security guard who spied him had also seen the same man two days before, dumpster-diving in the elementary school's refuse. When approached, the bum calmly explained he was hungry and didn't want to beg or bother anyone for a handout. He knew that hospitals and schools threw away lots of untouched food, and he'd survived on it for a long time. The guard told him that he couldn't continue eating out of the hospital's trash. It was unhealthy. The guard also warned that the man was trespassing. But, the sentry did feel bad for Martin, so he offered to bring him a tray of food. Supper was being served at the moment, he explained, and, if Martin could wait a minute, he could have a hot meal. Martin gratefully waited.

Unfortunately for Martin, the cafeteria worker who brought him the supper tray had worked in the Tacoma hospital where Martin had practiced, and recognized him. After delivering the tray, the young woman reported to the security guard that she was pretty sure the bum was actually Dr. Cochran. While Martin was still eating at the picnic table on the south side of the hospital building, the Morton police chief, his only deputy and the hospital security guard attempted to arrest him. They were a bit too slow, and Martin ran. He bolted across Temple Avenue, cut through some yards, and eventually dashed into the woods south of highway 12.

An all-out manhunt ensued. Local cops from

Longview, Centralia, Mossyrock, and even Tacoma, along with the SBI and the FBI, descended on the woods south of town. They combed the area between the hospital and Riffe Lake, but came up empty-handed. Somehow Martin had backtracked and headed north. He was captured the next day around Mineral Lake, quite by accident. Around noon, a fisherman and his Army Ranger son saw him cross the road. Staff Sgt. Stephen Tenner, 32, and a veteran of Desert Storm, chased a haggard Dr. Cochran down and tackled him alongside the highway. The younger Tenner put a 9mm Ruger to Martin's temple while his father hogtied the former Marine Corps hero. Martin didn't struggle after the tackle, and, in fact, complimented the sergeant on his speed and takedown skill.

"We'd heard about the manhunt on the radio, and the cops showed us a picture of the doctor when we went through a roadblock. 'Course the picture was how he *used* to look. But they gave us a good description of how he looked now. The bum running across the highway could only be him. I knew he was a killer and a desperate criminal, but I figured I could overpower him, and, of course, I had a gun . . . He was real nice to us, not angry at all. We actually had a pleasant conversation while we waited on the cops to arrive. We talked about fishing and sailing. He even told a couple of war stories. He was pretty hungry, so I fed him one of our tuna fish sandwiches," the *Tacoma Times* quoted Sergeant Tenner.

The FBI took control of Martin. He was whisked back to the Pierce County jail, where he stayed until he was extradited to South Carolina.

It took two full days to retrieve and digest all of the reports. I was exhausted, dry-mouthed and sweaty when I finished with all the video footage and print coverage. I felt hollow, like some pervert who enjoys reliving others' vulgar calamities, a psycho who's addicted to watching re-runs of the Manson family's murderous escapades, or the cannibalistic exploits of Jeffrey Dahmer. I felt alone and wished I could call Kelly. I missed her. The weight of our separation pressed on me even harder. My mind ricocheted between my marital troubles and Martin's. And I wondered if there existed a breaking point for everyone. What would it take for me to lose all control and become a monster? I prayed I'd never find out.

After two beers at the waterfront bar where I met Cindy's girlfriends, I dialed Adrienne's number. On the fourth ring, I hung up, thought about phoning Kat or Vic, but didn't. I had two more beers by myself at a dark corner table, ate a bowl of free pretzels while watching a silenced episode of X Games, and pondered Martin's plight, his descent into the abyss of madness. I tried to envision Cindy's daily struggle, her singular hell. My visions were shallow. I prayed for her.

I headed home the next morning.

12

Martin's Notebooks

I returned home and dug into Martin's notebooks as soon as I could. But first I had to deal with my own divorce mess. In the five months since I first learned of Martin Cochran, my life had taken a nose dive. It was hard to believe that I'd lost my job and marriage, while at the same time discovering a story that could potentially cure my journalistic slump and marital collapse. And it was frightening that during all of the bickering, I couldn't help but identify with the tormented doctor.

Lawyers have a unique way of frustrating clients and infuriating their adversaries. Each phone call, appointment, and court appearance with my attorney was costing me hundreds of dollars. Each impotent attempt to defend myself against Kelly's lawyer's attacks cost me thousands. In the dead of night, wrestling with sweaty sheets, I dreamed of revenge, or skipping the country. Was this how it all began for Martin?

I was being accused of things that'd never happened. The judge was led to believe I'd been unfaithful to Kelly while away from home investigating stories. At the very least, her lawyer insisted, I was uncaring. Kelly was left alone all too often, and, when I was at home, I made myself unavailable—sequestered in my office, supposedly working.

There were accusations of abandonment, frequent arguments, threats of physical violence, irreconcilable differences, and "who knows what" while I was "out on the road." I was flabbergasted. The truth was that Kelly and I did have arguments (like all married couples) and sometimes they became loud and heated, but we'd never gotten physical. She may have felt abandoned. I couldn't really help that. I paid as much attention to her as I could, but I did have to travel in order to investigate my assignments, and I did have to sequester myself in my office to write. Writing is what I do to pay the bills. I was sorry her real estate commissions dried up. Her lack of income had drained our accounts and had stolen her sense of worth. Her depression and drinking didn't help the situation. Finally, I was never unfaithful to my wife.

Do all divorce lawyers come up with the same crap? Was Kelly's attorney using the same template as Cindy's? Do judges really believe all of the garbage being slung around the courtroom? Hadn't they been representing one side or the other prior to becoming a judge? Don't they know the game? Or, is it just a game, and, in reality, nothing needs to be said. Each party will get about half, except the "woman" will get the bigger half *and* the kids—if there are any. What a joke! But I wasn't laughing.

It was brilliantly convenient that while I was in Tacoma, our lawyers had come to an agreement. All that was needed now were our two signatures. They'd even divvied up the spoils. Kelly would be awarded the house and a monthly alimony check, which amounted to one third of my former monthly wage. I would continue to pay for the house until it sold, and we'd split the profit 50/50. They also agreed that Kelly shouldn't be responsible for any of our accumulated debt. They agreed that she would receive half of my pension savings.

They'd even computed my probable earnings based on me working until age sixty-seven and a half, and decided how much of that Kelly was entitled to. Of course, it should be paid as a lump sum now. Plus, they agreed that I should pay all of Kelly's attorney's fees. I was livid! I couldn't believe the nerve of these people. It's a wonder some vessel in my head didn't explode.

I wasn't about to just roll over and take it in the shorts. I refused to sign. So, we went round and round in the lawyers' offices, on the phone, and in court. In the end things didn't change much. My lawyer proved to be worthless. Hers had more energy. It seemed the judge was clearly biased, taking sides with the "weaker gender." I couldn't help but reflect on Martin's divorce and the late Ms. Steele. My blood boiled. Sometimes murder crossed my mind.

I feared it might take months to finalize everything, but I couldn't afford to wait any longer. My savings were gone, and the credit cards maxed

After three weeks of wrangling, I gave my full attention to the notebooks. I needed to finish this project, publish *something*, and get a paycheck. I'd already skimmed through the binders. Mostly, Martin recorded his daily drudgery, but I'd seen many disturbing forays into a broken mind. Now, I read the diaries intently. I made notes. I looked for evidence of his alleged crimes. He didn't confess to anything. He *did*, however, leave some clues of misdeeds. And he railed against Cindy.

Martin had written for a dozen years. There were hundreds of pages to digest. I followed his journey. At first he seemed normal, but angry. As time passed, he seemed to slip deeper and deeper into a psychotic hole. His written words would expose his deteriorating mind.

170

In one chapter I copied some of his entries, I summarized several, and started where Martin did — with his first journal entry:

"I'm not sure why I am writing these words. The chaplain came by this evening. He brought in a few bibles, books, and writing materials. He even thought to bring some ink pens and a few postage stamps! He was a kind old fellow, wasn't nosey, didn't ask my name or a list of my crimes. He didn't press any religious philosophy. He only asked how we were all doing. Pastor McMinn. He is about seventy years old. I'll bet he's seen and heard everything. Nothing could surprise him. Most of the guys didn't say much, but I used the opportunity as a much needed diversion from the monotony of this eight man cage.

He gave me this notebook and pen. Anyway, I'm not sure what to write or what good it will do — except it'll be a diversion. BUT, who am I writing to? Myself? And what will I write about? My daily 'activities'? I've never kept a diary. Maybe I shall write a great novel which will be published posthumously and receive a prize. Or, maybe I'll write a lengthy confession of all my sins. Maybe I'll turn my soul inside out so future readers will understand the monster the child became, weaknesses exposed, secrets revealed, a broken heart avenged! The inner workings of a dreamer twisted by deceit, shafted by THE SYSTEM, dragged to the abyss and hurled into Hell. The carpet of LIFE literally snatched from underfoot creating another victim . . . maybe I'll just start with the fact that I've been in this cell for three and a half weeks (and it sucks) and my extradition hearing will be in two days. I guess I should get ready to go to South Carolina and I suppose I'll never be free again."

In the first entry, Martin went on to describe life in the Pierce County jail, a couple of the guards, how he had been treated and the food. It was interesting to note that he described all of this in fine detail, but only mentioned a couple of his cellmates. I wondered if he purposely omitted the others to avoid any conflicts should the pages be discovered.

He continued:

"This place is small — and it's grungy. I was a little surprised that 8 guys are crammed into a room that's maybe 12 ft X 15 ft. Of course, I wasn't expecting the Hilton. It looks like this cell was built for six, but two more bunks were added some time ago. You really have to stay on your bunk; otherwise you're standing too close to some other guy. No offense meant, but this place reeks. It smells like a high school football locker-room after the BIG GAME was lost — sweaty, urine stained jock straps, rotting fungus encrusted feet and greasy low-budget hamburger farts mixed with noxious Pine-Scented Lysol bathroom cleaner. The foul body odor of my new buds hangs in the dead air like the thick morning fog that paralyzes San Francisco, blinding all and threatening death just out of sight. The rancid B.O. takes second place only when one of a couple of my fine neighbors draw close to speak in hushed private tones. BAD BREATH from HELL! In all of my medical career, I've never encountered a more revolting stench: rotting Armadillo road kill — guts and brains spread across the pavement — broiling on an Arizona summer highway wetted with dying camel piss and mixed with the fetid gases emitted from the cesspools of open waste canals like those poisoning Calcutta. Guarded though they are, a smile displays swollen, reddened gums — on the verge of bleeding. Teeth broken and decaying (or missing), the juncture of teeth and gums a sickly slimy white and green bacterial soup slowly digesting the hopeless tissue.

This cell was once painted mustard yellow, I guess. Now, the walls and ceiling are a mucus greenish, baby shit-yellow, nicotine-stained color. There are multiple places where the old paint has peeled or worn away exposing the grey cement block or metal plating. Crudely etched offensive graffiti, dried buggers and old blood stains decorate the walls instead of Van Gogh prints or family portraits. The corners are all a gray black, dirt grime color. Apparently, not one among the hundreds of former inhabitants was a good housekeeper. Most offensive is the shower floor and the shitter.

The shower, probably an afterthought, stands next to the totally open-for-viewing toilet. There's a semi-transparent curtain that you can pull around a semicircular track to almost block depraved sex starved eyes while you are washing. The curtain is almost as nasty as the floor. The floor of the shower is poured concrete left coarse to provide sure footing. But, over the years the little grooves have filled in with soap scum, body oils, invincible green bacterial slime and fungi cultures, semen, and the nauseating pine cleaner.

The toilet is a simple bare industrial grade stainless-steel crapper. It's never been cleaned. The only way to guess that it's metal is that the area where you sit is polished (kinda) by people's asses. There's no lid. And while the rim displays a trace of metallic shine, the rest of the thing is totally disgusting! I refused to sit on it for two weeks. I couldn't bring myself to touch the foul shit catcher and I refused to let my balls hang down into the sewage pit. But finally, I surrendered to the hopelessness of the situation.

Now, I will only take a crap when I feel the turd emerging. My time in contact with the revolting affair is kept to an absolute minimum. And I hold my sack up so it doesn't drag in the poison. Gone are the days when I would sit, sip coffee and read the sports page while enjoying a leisurely dump. No!

There are things growing - that've been expelled - clinging to the walls of the septic port. The inner bowl resembles the shallow waters of a natural hot spring where furry green and brown slime and algae abound. It is putrid. Ancient shit splatter has turned black; the more recent is still brown. It probably stinks horribly, but is trumped by the afore mentioned B.O. and rotting feet funk. The exposed outside is stained brown and black and deep green. The filth is baked on, enameled, like desert wall varnish – a permanent part of the landscape. It would take a sandblaster to remove it.

I suppose that everybody would appreciate the john being cleaned but no one wants to be the bitch that does it.

The jolt you get when being thrown into a jail cell is like a bullet to the gut. At first you can't believe it. Life will never be the same again . . . The iron door slams closed. There could be a hundred killers inside the cell, but you are all alone, totally alone. Forever isolated from your former life, normal life, all of your loved ones. Any plans, any dreams. You are totally defenseless and at the mercy of your captors (just like Dai Phong – the bastards!)

The next assault is by your cellmates' eyes. They measure you. Examine you. Study your face and manner attempting to categorize you. Are you a threat to them? Are you the new alpha male or the new pussy? The latest bad ass with a hair trigger and a massive hard-on for anyone he can bend over, or the newest punk with a big mouth and an asshole to match. The new meat. I didn't feel super strong but hopefully didn't seem too freaked out. I walked in with my head up and my eyes meeting everyone else's. I was the Marine, the Vietnam Vet, the Doctor – the murderer."

I was surprised by Martin's vulgar language. I'd expected words befitting a scholar, erudite phrases and imagery, but Martin's notes exposed his core: a rough and tumble upbringing, a brutish combat veteran and resurgence of base survival mentality. Martin's first journalistic efforts reflect a fairly sane man. There's a little humor mixed with the harsh reality of life behind bars. Nowhere, in these first pages, is there an indication of a mind gone astray, warped with anger and revenge, capable of horrific acts against his former lover, the mother of his beloved child.

He wrote on:

"I guess I didn't threaten anyone or invite trouble. I'm staying firm and calm. I haven't had any ENCOUNTERS yet. And at this point, I'm the 3rd senior guy and maybe the oldest. "Red" might be older. It's hard to tell. He's got way more gray hair than me and way less teeth. His face has about 10 times the wrinkles as mine. No matter how old he is, he's definitely been rode hard and put up wet many more times than I have. Even though I haven't been here that long, about a dozen other upstanding, totally innocent citizens have come and gone in these few weeks. And I'll be on my way soon. So far, thank God, there's been no funny business. I do wonder what my next home will be like. A change of scenery might be nice – but maybe not! Lights out. Good night Martin."

The next day he wrote:

"Restless night. Too much smoke in the air – even though they're not supposed to smoke after lights out. Oh well, what can you expect out of a bunch of criminals? Anyway, I was describing some of the stuff around here. Returning to the bathroom theme: one of the worst parts of being here is the lack of privacy. Eight guys in a 15 X 12 and nothing between you on the shitter and them. I learned quickly to drop my pants and drape my front. We have to wear this one piece orange

coverall that zips from the neck to the crotch. You've got to unzip all the way and peel the top part in order to expose your ass to take a crap. I wrap the shirt part around my thighs and try to keep it from touching the nasty-ass floor or the filthy shitter. Eyes follow your every move, some twinkle with amusement – the awkwardness of your exposed, vulnerable situation. Some openly stare, obviously interested in what you're covering up. And most everyone hoots or whistles when you rip a loud one or spew chunks with explosive force. How nasty. Plus, of course, there's a couple of cameras on the ceiling recording everything. Can you imagine being the guy who watches everybody wiping their ass and pulling their cock?

Let's turn to something more pleasant. Hmmm, there isn't anything.

But, Martin went on to describe his hum-drum daily life behind bars and the miserable food. He ended his second day's entry with a description of two guards, one was his favorite, and the other was a female who was fat, scruffy, and abusive.

"She could use a little Chevy Van attitude adjustment!" he wrote.

And he briefly entertained his anxiety regarding his extradition hearing scheduled the next day, writing: *"Wonder what will happen tomorrow? I'm fairly certain I'll be taking a little trip south soon. Sure hope the rednecks are as civil as us Great North Westerners."*

His third journal note began as the second did:

"Another restless night, full of tossing and turning. And the new guy didn't help. He was drunk and pissed off. He was literally thrown into the cell around midnight. He cussed the cops, his ex-wife, the 'System', God and the saints for about an hour until Thompson (the guard) threatened him with a Tazer

176

and solitary. Curry and Coones (hard dick recidivists) threatened death. He's lucky that he settled down cause I'll bet Coones wasn't kidding.

Anyway, in a few minutes, I'll be taken to the courtroom for the extradition hearing. How bizarre! Two years ago I walked through hallways, my status clearly marked by a flapping white coat and the stethoscope around my neck. I had value. I was somebody! Today, I'll be led through high security back hallways, hidden – a filthy malignant pustule in the ass crack of society. There will be a guard in front and one behind our little parade. I'll be chained to other pustules in handcuffs and leg irons. I think I'll wear my bright orange jump suit.

Later that day he penned:

Whew! What a morning. My hearing took about ten minutes, but we all had to sit on that wooden bench all morning with our leg irons shackled to a logging chain running under it. Very uncomfortable. We (seven of us) were parked on the bench for 45 minutes before court began. And we sat until each of us was dealt with and court was adjourned for lunch at 1:30. The only time I could move around was when I was called in front of the judge. The State of Washington could see no reason to delay or prevent my transfer to the great state of South Carolina to answer charges of murder. So, I'll be southbound ASAP!

For the first eight months, Martin recorded the date and time of his entries, but for some reason, after that he mostly stopped. He would sometimes mark the date or indicate it by saying things like, *"It's Christmas,"* or *"Thanksgiving,"* or *"Marcus' birthday."* He *did* record important dates such as: *"Murder Trial, Day 1"* and *"DAY ONE on DEATH ROW."*

Also, now and then, he would record how many days he'd been incarcerated, or how long it had been since he had seen Marcus. I think that he just got tired of thinking about how long he'd been jailed and how long it would be until the end—whatever that meant. So, I was able to follow the sequence of log entries for the most part.

During all of those years, most of the writings were simple. Martin recorded his routines, meals, and exercise rituals. But, sometimes, he wrote lengthy tomes on subjects ranging from memories of the war, to adventures in the mountains, or of sailing. He forwarded his philosophies and wrote quite a number of poems. And, as you could expect, he sometimes raged against Cindy and her cohorts, or he would rant about *"THE SYSTEM."*

His first three days of writing seemed to be a comforting diversion, full of sick or humorous descriptions and a little anxiety. But, after the third day, he didn't record anything for the next three days. He was being extradited. Finally, in the Richland County jail, Martin found his voice again:

What a fucked up, stinking hole! And what a bunch of fucked up, stinking assholes! These rednecks really are shit-heads! It has taken three days for the bastards to 'inventory' my stuff. So I've had no change of clothes, no soap, no toothbrush. I did get one threadbare sheet, one blanket, a two-inch thick, thoroughly used-up mattress complete with rust stains, Dollar Store flip flops and one condom! I'm in an isolation cell (6'X8'- hell if ya ain't crazy when they throw you in here ya will be in 15 minutes) until they can determine if I'm stable enough to be in a cage with others. How long will that take? I asked in-take sergeant. Who knows, was his reply. GREAT!

I'm mad as hell as you can tell. (WHO YA TALKIN TO MARTIN?) . . . well at least I've got my stuff back now and I can brush my teeth and write about it.

The ride back to SC wasn't too bad. I flew Delta, escorted by two of the nicest gentlemen. I stayed cuffed to Sgt. Damon Morris except when I was in the pisser in Denver. Then, I was put in leg irons before being uncuffed. The other guard's name was Smitty. The Sergeant was a goliath of a man and black as coal. His brilliant white eyes and teeth were like some cartoon Negro in the 1930s. He had oily skin and shoulders that barely fit into the plane – they both rubbed against the overhead compartments as he walked down the aisle with his head bent low. I guess he must be 6'6' and 315. The worst part was that Morris needed two seats and I needed one, but we always sat on the two seat side of the planes and I had to sit on the window side. The Sgt. barely fit and I didn't fit at all. Sgt. Morris was dressed in DOC blues with all of the appropriate regalia: spiffy military style hat, name plate and patches and gleaming Florsheim leathers. Smitty must've been with the SBI/FBI/CIA/NASA/secret agent undercover branch of the judicial system. He was dressed in a gray tweed suit, nondescript black leather dress shoes, no tie. No evidence of being a cop. Very quiet and always a few feet away. Behind me. They treated me like a killer! Oh yeah . . . Well, I wouldn't kill them. Neither man spoke very much, but they answered my questions politely and didn't pry into my situation."

Life in the Richland County jail was different. Its clientele seemed rougher, poorer, and mostly black. After the isolation cell, Martin was moved into a 20' x 20' cage, along with ten other men. It featured a small, opaque, barred window that leaked dirty sunlight into the cell.

One improvement was that inmates were allowed to exercise outdoors for one hour each day. Another improvement was that the toilet/sink combo was pretty clean. And while he still didn't like to sit on it, Martin complimented his new roommates on their attention to cleanliness. The menu, while lacking in protein and portion size, was rich in fat. He described it as:

"*. . . fried chicken, chicken fried steak, gravy on mashed potatoes, gravy on white rice, grits and gravy, biscuits and gravy, and chunks of fatback in mushy greens . . . You gotta' love Southern cookin'!*"

Martin spent twenty months in Richland County jail. Then, he was sent to Lieber Correctional Institution and placed on death row after being convicted of first degree murder. While in the county jail, life was much more colorful. Inmates came and went, though not as frequently as in the Washington state jail. In the Richland cell, there were prisoners awaiting trials, and there were several who were serving entire sentences.

During the almost two years Martin spent in the county jail, he shared the cell with six other men who were being held on murder charges.

A couple of days after being transferred into the larger cell, Martin wrote:

"*I guess it's better here. We go outside once a day to exercise. We can shower every third day and they're cleaner than in Tacoma. There we showered every other day but the stall was nasty, as I've already said. Here the shower isn't in our cell. There are four faucets in the head so four guys are in there at the same time. Like boot camp. The water is turned on for five minutes and it's little more than a trickle but it's pretty warm. And, of course, there's a guard standing just outside and ceiling mounted cameras. No hanky panky now boys! Hell I don't mind anymore. See me naked – watch me*" *shit — nothing really matters anymore. Anyway I don't have a choice.*

Right now I'm one of three guys in this cell accused of murder. The other two are innocent. One's wife 'musta runned off' and the other's story is 'some other dude did it — I wasn't even there that night.' A couple of guys are here for drugs, one guy is serving 30 days for drunk and disorderly . There's a couple of innocent thieves awaiting trial. One crazy asshole who, 'ain't got no idea ah why I's here.' And one empty bunk. I kinda like a couple of them. We play cards most of the day and swap bullshit stories, but I'm always on edge with the murderers and that crazy fucker."

Martin had no chance to exercise while locked up in Tacoma, but in Richland he started an exercise program while out in the yard:

"A glorified dog run, 33 strides long by 21 strides wide. The broken concrete and sand lot is surrounded by a double cyclone fence 12 ft high, each fence topped with razor wire. The fences are about four feet apart and the outer one is supposedly electrified! At least that's what the little yellow and black signs warn."

Here he drew lightening bolts zapping the behind of an escaping prisoner.

During the twenty months in Richland, Martin gained some weight, due to his rich diet and exercise program. He looked forward to his daily regimen. The yard offered welcome relief from the cramped cell:

"The yard has been a godsend. I dream of it. Despite the fences, concertina wire and high voltage, mocking crows perched between razors and hungry for my eyes, I feel a tiny slice of freedom there."

But it could be a dangerous place, too. Detainees from other cells used the yard at the same time as Martin and his cellmates. Sometimes there were twenty-five guys in the arena. And sometimes tensions ran high.

The funny business he'd avoided in the Tacoma county jail finally caught up to him shortly after he arrived in South Carolina. But he didn't expound on the event until years later. Instead, in a passage dated three months after being transferred to Richland, Martin simply jotted, *". . . and I got a pretty good workout with B.B. yesterday. In the hole for two weeks, but worth it."*

Five years later he explained the "workout" and the reason he'd been in the hole:

"Remember Big Bad in county? The word was he would fuck me up Tuesday . . . 'Take the doctor down' – 'the punk who messed up his wife – a woman!'

BAD IDEA BIG BAD!

. . . Came around the corner with his boys in tow. He postured up, Charles Atlas arms across his chest. His boys blocked the guard's camera view and then an evil laugh, 'So ya like to hurt girls. Huh - DOCTOR?'

Uh oh – better be ready Big Bad. I got a little somethin' special for ya. An entire five gallon bucket of bad ass, Marine Corps dirty tricks whup ass!

He stood there straight and tall, imposing – massive arms, nasty prison tattoos, long curly hippie hair and Fu Manchu – black eyes full of hate. I could feel his intent. He was about to unleash some prison justice.

Stood a little too close. (Zone One, perfect!) Waited a second too long.

I broke the stare down, dropped my eyes, focused on the target . . . raised my hands to my face as I meekly let out a little, 'Oh no, I didn't . . .' And then, instantly, explosively, violently – with all of my force, totally committed, I shot my hands up high (as a diversion) and shouted, 'FUCK YOU!' while I front kicked his nuts into Georgia.

Now this is an old trick with a twist: appear intimidated, use a visual and auditory diversion to confuse the opponent momentarily, then ATTACK!

The front kick to the balls bent him over forward, so I grabbed two fistfuls of hair and slammed his face into my knee. Blood shot out his nose and he dropped like the proverbial sack of spuds. In that instant, I swarmed him — kept hold of that nasty hair and twirled around onto his back, locked my legs around his middle and squeezed all the air out of him. I moved my arms to the death choke position and squeezed until he passed out. (Here's the twist) — I'd sharpened my fingernails to little points. It wasn't much, but the best I could do on short notice. BIG BAD was O-U-T. He was mine and so I gave him a little somethin' to think about: opened up his eyelids with my left hand and dug into his eyes with my sharpened nails — I got 'em pretty good. He definitely wouldn't be fighting any more that day.

The two goons were taken by surprise, but they came at me pretty quick, gave me a couple kicks — one in the head and one in my back. But I held onto BIG BAD, rolled in the dirt and used him as a shield until the guards broke us up.

BIG BAD came to. He was a bloody mess and he started crying in pain and about being blind (awh, how sad!). His nose was obviously broken.

My knee felt busted too — but it wasn't. I did get a big purple hematoma around my ear and bruises on my back from being kicked. I got a little punishment time in a cell all by myself — locked down for two weeks. BIG BAD got a trip to the hospital. A nose job and eye patches. I heard he was nearly blinded and his vision never returned to normal. Breaks my heart. *Maybe it's not a good idea to pick on a trained KILLER. Thanks, USMC."*

Martin clearly relished the memory of besting Big Bad. He even illustrated the page, drawing a hand with sharpened fingernails and a likeness of his opponent with natty hair, eye patches and a broken, bloodied nose.

While in the hole for assaulting Big Bad, all alone with no diversion except his writings, Martin confronted himself:

"How has it come to this? In a 6 x 9 cage, pen and paper my only friend. My pride. MY PRIDE! Pride has led to too many downfalls. Kings and commoners alike. Should there be anything so important that you exchange your entire life, your freedom for it? Family. But what happens when one of the family becomes the enemy? Cindy traded family for a fuck. She traded blue skies and warm currents for a lightning storm. I could have simply walked away. I should have walked away, I wouldn't be here now. But, Marcus. My son. I would have walked away from my son, my flesh and blood. What would he have grown up believing? What story would Cindy have told? Would Trip have become his father? Why is all of that so important? Does any of that matter now? NO! They're all dead. I'm dead. Why must I be a fighter? It was obvious what and who she wanted. Why not just let it be. Why fight for something that's broken? Pride forced action. I am a man of action. The other side of the coin is ugly. It has to be for survival's sake. Pride is ugly, war is ugly, killing is ugly. I am ugly!"

A couple of weeks after Martin got out of the hole he was called to the warden's office again. This time to be informed he'd soon be transferred to Albany to face charges of kidnapping Cindy, and aggravated assault with intent to kill.

In Albany, Martin was held in solitary. He simmered in a 6' x 9' airless, basement cell for seven weeks, and he wrote more about Cindy than he ever had. The most chilling amounted to a written assault. On the top half of a page he wrote over and over:

"THAT CHEATING BITCH! THAT SNEAKING PIECE OF SHIT! WHORE!"

Then:

"Why did I let her live? She deserves death . . . they all did. I know Martin, I know. There are things worse than death and she got it. But still it would've felt nice to have choked the life out of the fucking little whore, watched her lips turn purple as she fought for her life—and failed. Why didn't I just end it all there? Maybe even turned the tables on myself . . .?"

Martin illustrated this page with evil symbols, and Cindy's face with devil's horns, blood dripping from her eyes. He drew a bleeding, broken heart pierced by a knife. And he penciled a menacing black cloud with the hand of God gripping a lightning bolt. It was stabbing a naked woman's crotch. Cindy?

The entry that followed this tirade made my jaw drop. It was the first time that Martin showed his truly vicious, calculating, homicidal side:

"Oh, for a knife! I'll never forget the feel of a solid knife in my hand—the weight of the weapon, the lines of the blade. To be one with a silent killer—the handle: sensuous, fitted to my hand. The blade—strong, sharp, deadly—begging to be plunged deep, deep, violently, silently, murderously deep into tender, vulnerable throat flesh or ripping through lungs and heart and great vessels. I dream of my K-Bar. Stout. Black. Death in a sheath. Power. Murder. Silent . . . remember Khe Sahn?—that poor bastard who thought I was dead? The fuck-

er bent down close to my face to see if I was breathin'. Not a good idea. Dumb ass — should have kicked me in the face or shot me in the head — HA! Stick your face in mine and I'll kill ya. God it felt good to sink the K-Bar into his throat! He was scared shitless. Blood everywhere. His eyes told the story: shock and surprise. I have FUCKED UP MAJORLY! . . . and now I'm going to die. I laughed my ass off. Face to face. His blood sprayed all over me. Pain and LIFE gushed out his neck. His slanted eyes popped to the size of dinner plates. He gurgled and tumbled before he could pull the trigger.

Yeah and in Duc Tho. Plunged the ole' K Bar into Chuckie's supraclavicular sweet spot – the best! Left Carotid, Supraclavicular, Innominate, Jugular, Aortic arch, Vagus, Phrenic nerves---God what a treasure trove of instant death. Did I bag the atria or ventricle? I know I got the lung. Bubbles. Bubbles of blood. I wish it hadn't been so dark so I could have seen his eyes better. Remember Thornton's?"

The first time I read the passage, I put down the journal. The imagery was too much. My blood froze and the nape of neck crackled.

Many questions raced through my mind: Were all military personnel trained to think this way or only Marines? Could *I* have been trained to think like that? Did you have to think like that in order to survive during war? Did stressful divorces trigger the same neurons as hand-to-hand combat?

The list went on: Would things have been different had Martin never been to war or killed face-to-face? Had Martin simply reverted to instinctive battle tactics? Had he been hiding this penchant for killing his whole life? Was he a homicidal maniac before he met Cindy?

I couldn't believe the savagery, the evil intent, and the cruel joy Martin experienced as he saw the life drain out of his enemy.

Another short entry highlighted Martin's cruel heart. It was Cindy's birthday. He drew a heart with the date inside and a caption, *"It's your B'DAY CINDY so don't just sit around all day! . . . oh, that's right you're paralyzed. That's all ya can do . . . Ain't that a shame. Life can be such a bitch."*

When I read that one, I had to shake my head. Each time our decorated war hero, our hard-working betrayed provider, our grieving childless father crowed about his triumph over Cindy, the miniscule amount of sympathy I had for him slipped closer toward zero.

I continued with his physical journey through the legal system and his mental unraveling. In the Albany basement confines, Martin's moods swung wildly. He was lonely and depressed. He became irate with the system and his legal counsel. His madness intensified. He became passionately vicious.

Another entry:

"Haven't written in a few days. Too dark down here, dark, DARK, ALMOST BLACK!! Too damn dark. Might as well be blind, nothing to see anyway and nothing to say. Nothin that's worth shit. I've done a lot of push ups and sit ups. The only thing bad about that is the sweat. No air down here and a shower every third day. NASTY. The orange onpiece must be made out of plastic — it doesn't breathe. So I hang out all day in my skivvies otherwise too damn hot and clammy. Nobody, nobody around — too lonely & quiet, just depressed — too down for my own good. Where is that fuckin lawyer? He was supposed to be here three days ago. Get me

out of this cell and chat in some interrogation room – maybe with a window. Air for sure. Coffee? Piece of shit I ain't saying nothing. No wait, the more I talk the longer we lounge around in the fat-cat room. Baffle em with bullshit. Drag it out . . . way out . . . Hey here comes somebody."

That somebody was the lawyer, Richard Edward Strupp III. The entry continued:

"...18 years old, all pimply faced, probably still a virgin. Says my best defense is to plead. Probably get 5 to 15 for kidnapping and 15 to 35 for attempted 1st degree murder pleaded down to aggravated assault and drop the auto theft."

But Martin did not get out of his cell for the brief interview and he was left fuming:

"The fuckers, the assholes! Didn't let me out of this hole to talk with pimple face. We had to chat in here. And zit boy only spent 30 minutes discussing 'the case.' He had a pressing appointment with another client. Probably some hot little whore who'll be thanking him for his services by providing some of hers. He says he'll be back tomorrow and we'll go over the rest of the case. THE REST? I barely got finished with how the bitch did me dirty when ZB flew out of here."

He railed against the SYSTEM and ZB (zit boy, a.k.a. R.E. Strupp III, Attorney at Law) for the rest of the page. He ended this diatribe with:

". . . well the best part of this whole damn mess – and I forgot about it until just now – is that I have the right to face my accuser! Oh, my beautiful former paramour, my sweet little ex-wife, the mother of my former alive child, the lying – cheating whore who ruined my life and stole my happiness. I get to face her. And delight of all delights – I get to witness the results of my Chevy Van instant karma! Even if someone, somehow, made some improvements to her formerly angelic face that somehow became so monstrously disfigured . . . I'll

get the orgasmic pleasure of seeing her wheeled in and pointing me out with no fingers!!! Well I think that she'll still have one. Wasn't it the middle one on her right hand? Shit. I did leave three on her L hand . . . OOPS! What happened to your wedding ring finger, Cindy? DISARTICULATED? You say? Well that was just plain mean, now wasn't it"?

The following day, Mr. Strupp returned and recommended a plea bargain. Martin recorded that he wasn't about to plead guilty. He wanted a long, drawn-out trial. He wanted to see Cindy squirm for a week or two.

The trial lasted three days. Cindy never showed. Martin was furious, he threw a tantrum. He drew a half-page likeness of Cindy's face and attacked it. He punished the page, stabbed and gouged it, dug into it with the tip of his pen. He raged at the portrait like it was Cindy herself. He wrinkled the page, squeezing the life out of her neck, and punctured the paper in many places, especially her eyes.

"No Cindy!! (the usual profuse use of demeaning expletives) *It would have been better — more fun — to have sliced her up into pieces in the van and watch her die slowly, painfully, begging for mercy. Starved her for days and then fed her with her own flesh! I was too kind. Anesthesia during torture! Antibiotics. Hemostasis. What a pussy I was! . . . Where is my JUSTICE?? Where is my son? Where is my reason to live?"*

It seemed that after the fit, Martin tried to smooth out the page and he either shed tears that smeared some of the ink, or he may have spit on his drawing. In any event, the page had been marred by liquid, and the pages that followed were basically ruined. But he left them in place — four sheets — pockmarks , rips, and all.

I discovered, while reading through the trial's transcripts, that Cindy's absence was due to her need for further surgery. She was hospitalized and unable to travel from Springfield to Albany.

On the final page Martin penned, *"Sentenced today. Back to SC soon. Don't feel like writing."*

He was sentenced to at least twenty-seven years and sent back to South Carolina to await trial for murdering Thornton. He recorded nothing for a while, but finally, in a new spiral bound he wrote:

"Haven't felt like writing. Been two months since Albany. Can't wait for the next go round. At least I'm back in GP (general population). *Crowded, stinky, noisy, fucked up, but better than solitary in the basement. Play cards and watch TV with 4 other sewer rats for now. Try not to focus on the bitch. Ommm.*

The next "go round" saw Martin with new counsel. "Heckle & Jeckle," the public defenders who represented him during his arraignment, were replaced by Terrance Smith and Alexis Brock. Smith was a veteran of six years and Brock had been with the Public Defenders Office for just fourteen months. They had worked together on only one capital case. Smith had represented eleven men accused of murder, and Brock only one. All defendants had been found guilty — most had plea bargained. Nine men received life sentences, and two were ordered to pay with their lives.

Martin didn't like the new counselors any better than the first two, but he *did* appreciate the female's figure, smooth skin, and perfume. They interviewed him three months after his return to Richland County jail.

"*Smith's tired of the legal game, but Brock is still enthusiastic. He's probably in this early 40s and she's in her late twenties.*

Plead guilty to 1st degree murder in exchange for life in prison — instead of death by lethal injection. They say. But, I don't want to spend any more time in this stinking place than I have to. There are things worse than death . . . right Cindy? You whore. No, I told em. Let's see what the State has got. Let's test your skills as DEFENDERS! Argue! Come on people use your training. Where are your balls? Oh yeah, MISS Brock. Well anyway, let's shoot it out — I ain't scared. Lethal injection was my job — only I always (well usually) brought em back. Shit, you just go to sleep and wake up in hell. It can't be as bad as a good old fashioned gas chamber or hanging or prison rape or divorce or shitty marriage. Come on COUNSELORS!"

The lawyers acquiesced to Martin's demand to plead innocent and force a trial. It took eleven months to prepare Martin's defense. But finally, the big day arrived.

"*Murder Trial Day 1*

Bozos & assholes, clowns and pricks. The Honorable T.S. Sherman II looks like porky pig in a robe. He slept in his car last night and didn't stop drinking until — well he didn't. Rudolf nosed bastard. Irritable cuss. Loves to bang that gavel. 'ORDER, ORDER IN THE COURT!' I'll order ya up something fat boy — a little tennis club smack on the head and a Wilson Pro Staff necktie. Wonders why the defendant didn't plead guilty? Cause I want my due process under the law, your honor. Pissed him off. Recess until tomorrow. Counselors, I'll see you in my chambers now."

The trial lasted four days. Martin said nothing throughout that time. The circumstantial evidence was convincing. The jury took only three hours to reach a verdict: guilty.

"Sentencing tomorrow. Can't wait. Very nervous. What will LIFE BEHIND BARS be like? How long will that be? How long until THE INJECTION? Some guys have been on death row forever! That's a long time. Suicide? Hmmm."

His next entry read:

"Well, at least the suspense is over. Death by lethal injection. I'll be taking a ride to the big house and get a private room. How nice . . . how long?"

After twenty months in Richland County jail—including the few weeks up in Albany—Martin was transferred to Broad River Capital Punishment Facility. He got a private room complete with one, one hundred watt, totally enclosed, light bulb that was turned on every morning at five, and off every night at ten thirty.

There was no window to the outside world, only a ten-inch by four-inch, bulletproof Plexiglas pane in the solid steel cell door. The cell was six feet wide and eight feet deep with walls eight feet high. He got his own, private, stainless steel toilet and attached sink combo. His bunk was standard-issue, metal shelf with a thin, used, cotton-batting mattress and an emaciated foam pillow. Ancient white sheets, dishwater grey and stained from who knew what. The bed linens were washed every two weeks, and he never received the same ones twice. The meals and their timing were the same as any other jail.

At first, Martin was one of thirteen men on South Carolina's Death Row. By the time he was executed, he had twenty-three neighbors who were all scheduled to share his fate. Through the years, the names and faces of the staff changed and nine of the inmates were put to death. But, other than that, not much else ever changed. Death Row is regimented, tightly controlled, lonely, depressing, and very, very boring.

He wrote:

"It's the boredom and lack of human contact that's the worst part of the sentence. The knowledge that I'll one day be killed is worrisome, but the seclusion is more painful."

Seclusion and boredom drove Martin even crazier.

"At first I craved a little alone time, away from all the crazies in GP. But now, it would be nice to have some company. Some asshole to argue with, a scum bag to make fun of or play cards with. Any diversion would be nice. 18 months without commotion and only visited by the Chaplain and counted by guards. BORING."

A couple of pages later:

"Silence may be golden, but round here it's deafening and maddening. I've read the Bible – cover to cover 3 times! And it's not that interesting. Would be better if the guards would discuss it a bit. The Chap will. We've had some good discussions, but he wants to focus on forgiveness and I on Old Testament Payback. Otherwise . . . boring, boring, boring!

Boredom is a form of Death
Endless nothingness
Its tentacles steal your mind
Murder your thoughts
Squeeze the life from your dreams
Drain energy, drown creativity
Numb the brain like opium
A curtain colorless and lethal"

Six months later Martin opened up even more.

"How disturbing. Depressing. Today I'm down. Down, down, down! I've been so strong for so long, but today I am

weak. A coward. A pussy. Woe is me . . . why? Why would today be any different than any other da — than the 743 days before? Why would I feel down, depressed, sorry, worried. I know I can do the time. Piece of cake — just ignore TIME . . . somehow I HAVE LOST SIGHT of the MISSION and the SUCCESS and THE COST. It was worth it! Was it? I traded everything to settle a score. Revenge! I am dead without being dead. SHE lives . . . granted in misery I hope. But free to breathe the fresh air, to see a friend, go to the shore, to visit the grave. My son. My son. My Marcus — he's dead, dead, dead. I never took him to Alaska or a museum. There were so many things that I wanted us to share. Cindy IS responsible. Today I can not ignore it. I hold her accountable — to blame. The UNIVERSE said that she must pay! I followed orders."

The longer Martin sat in seclusion on Death Row, the more depressed and darker his entries became. They were snapshots into a mind that had become (even before prison) a vicious juggernaut, lethal, driven by revenge, fueled by deceit and hatred. Occasionally, he found enough sanity to record intelligent, sensitive, insightful thoughts, but as time dragged on most reflected his spiral into lunacy.

As I studied the journals, attempting to arrange those examples in a cohesive, interesting fashion that adequately reflected Martin's polarized mind, I found myself rising and falling along with him. And it was particularly disturbing when my own divorce issues dragged me into angry, dark places where I felt like following his lead, seeking revenge against Kelly.

My worst moment occurred when I answered the door to find two policemen waving an arrest warrant in my face. They said I had been accused of breaking into Kelly's car, stealing various items — including her purse from the trunk and using her credit cards. I was livid! I argued with them, but lost the verbal match. They handcuffed me and drove me uptown, where I spent the night in jail. I got out the next day after a call to my lawyer and laying out another five hundred dollars that I didn't have.

I sat in my study for quite some time, furious and worrying, but finally returned to my task. Unfortunately, Martin's next journal entry exacerbated my angry thoughts. It sent me into a tailspin. I wished I hadn't read it.

"I fucking hate her! In my heart, deep down in my soul! Every fiber of my being! Forever. Forever. Without regret. Without concession. Without remorse. She deserves the absolute worst of life. Whatever that may be. Torture, pain, humiliation, hopelessness. Burning, searing, singular, black, demented, beyond imagination agony, unending, never ending, eternal. Beyond description. PAIN. I truly hate her! And I know that I will pay for it. I must pay. She begs for it. God demands it. The UNIVERSE requires it! I will pay . . . gladly. You got what you deserve bitch! I'll accept the consequences."

I slapped the notebook shut and took a walk. It was a rainy, gloomy day, and my spirits were not lifted. When I returned home there was a message on my answering machine: "Hey Pierre. Sorry about the mix-up, turns out my car was one of several broken into in the neighborhood. They caught the guys this morning. Oh, and I found my purse in the pantry closet."

My head about exploded. No apology, no offer to reimburse me the five-hundred bucks. I phoned my lawyer. He was no help either, and the call probably cost me another hundred. Vengeance and schemes and escape routes spun round and round in my mind. I felt sick, close as I'd ever been to crazy. I drank a beer and decided, as I stared out the window at the rain, I'd had enough of Martin's meanness. I'll give you some examples of his other "sides," and wrap up this story.

Like many prisoners, Martin read the Bible and wrestled with some of its concepts.

"Blessed are the meek: for they shall inherit the earth." Matt. 5

No, the BOLD – criminals, shysters, lawyers and kings shall take what they please. The meek shall be served up for dinner with roasted carrots, a flagon of wine and a toast to strength and avarice. The meek will be annihilated, their flesh will fatten infants. Warriors will inherit the earth. Bad, mean, immoral men will reign until they totally consume each other. And in the end, the last bad ass standing will surrender his crown to Time. And TIME will inherit the earth.

The MEEK – they're just pathetic, gullible losers.

* * *

Oh yes, I told Marzocchi (the Chaplain) *– I think I know how He felt. Thorns and nails and nearly flogged to death is exactly what it feels like to have your only son stolen and killed. I know betrayal. Yes I do. My Judas is Cindy and her co-conspirator, Thornton. My life was torn away. My heart was ripped apart. My soul has been forsaken and damned to eternal misery. There was a purpose in His torment. There was meaning! A showy torture and crucifixion, lots of blood and silent suffering. The underdog, quiet and unassuming, bullied and beaten by the almighty authorities, yet preaching love and granting forgiveness with His final breaths. Onlookers aghast! Publicly murdered to grab attention, to drive home a point. Don't mess with Caesar. And . . . ah yes! The miracle of His gruesome murder – God's gift to mankind –*

196

His Son's Blood! The blood of forgiveness. Drink deep My children and celebrate in Heaven for all eternity. But ME — ME! My death will have no meaning. I will fade into the darkness of nothingness. My existence will have been pointless. The miracle of my birth inane. I would rather have been Jesus or even Judas! Marzocchi simply listened to me ramble on and on until the lights went out.

Another example of Martins keen intellect:

"Consider: at some moment in the distant past (a billion years ago?) a bunch of disparate atoms got together for some reason, bonded in such a fashion that from that moment forth the earth would never be as it had been only one moment before. These atoms, these molecules no longer simply existed, to be blown by the winds, stirred by the currents or frozen and thawed by the earth's orientation to the sun. These simple elements: carbon, nitrogen, hydrogen, oxygen, iron . . . formed a relationship that ACTED, that INTERACTED. At that moment, the precursors of 'US' were born! Simple chemistry? Advanced chemistry? LUCK? . . . COSMIC INTENTION? The union of those particles would one day give rise to all LIFE on Earth! They were the seeds from which sprang: Amino acids, Enzymes, DNA, Protozoa, Algae, Worms, Shrimp, Whale, Dinosaur, Monkey . . . MAN! They were the first step toward the most wondrous phenomenon in the universe: LIFE! Their bonds would transcend simple existence. They would ultimately allow not only LIFE, but also consciousness! . . . A few simple atoms, arranged in a very specific pattern yielding structures that create electrical potentials, produce energy, self replicate, communicate. Muscles, bones, nerves. Electricity in our bodies! Electric signals that allow us to walk, to talk, to think, to dream, to reflect on our place in the Universe, to investigate our own inner workings!"

There were examples of Martin's sensitivity and introspection:

"Once, I was a child, brand new, innocent. In Mother's arms, snug against her bosom, the womb of her lap, Heaven ! Protected, cherished; I was a miracle.

Once, I was a boy, on my Father's knee. He bounced me and sang about riding little horses and gum drop treats. He would whisper in my ear little secrets that we would keep . . . Mothers' birthday gift, or chewing gum in his dresser drawer. He was a giant. My hero. Indestructible. Omnipotent.

Once, I was a warrior, young, strong, disciplined. A Marine, a leatherneck, a devil dog, proud, determined, a defender of our country and freedom.

Once, I was a doctor, a healer. Smart, ambitious, tireless. A scientist, an alchemist, an artist, a magician.

Once, I was a lover. Passionate, giving, trusting. A believer. Deceived.

Once, I was a Father, a parent, proud, present, amazed, overjoyed. Hopeful.

Once, I was a friend.... to Vic, to Dan and Lou and all . . . to Cindy . . . where are they? Well . . .

Now, I am a prisoner. A criminal, a caged monster, a murderer, sequestered, ostracized, a ghost, a dead man walking. Threatened with death, promised poison. Hated. Hopeless. Dead already.

Once, I was Martin. Where have you gone, Martin?

'Once there was a way to get back home, once there was a way to get back HOME! Sleep little darling do not cry and I will sing a lullaby . . . boy you're gonna carry that weight, carry that weight a long time, boy you're gonna carry that weight, carry that weight a long time!' McCartney?

The weight is getting heavier. The long time is getting longer. I'm tired, really tired. When will it end? When will I go home? I'm tired.

* * *

I really can't remember what FREEDOM is like. You know the old saying that you don't know what you've got till it's gone. How true! Sometimes I can almost feel it — like a memory of your early childhood or your grandmother who died when you were five. Intellectually you know about it but you really can't feel it anymore. I have gotten close sometimes — when my eyes were shut and I can't see the walls or when I used to be allowed outside in 'the yard'. Now, these walls have become a part of me. They are almost like my skin — an ever present boundary. I have found some freedom in reading books. I've probably read every interesting book in this prison's library — some two or three times. In these six years, I've read the bible three times even though it's not that interesting. 'Now the Lord is the Spirit and where the Spirit of the Lord is, there is freedom.' I'll have to take it for now.

My freedom will come at the end of the white-light tunnel. "

And after nearly twelve years in prison, Martin recorded:

"FM (Father Mario Marzocchi — the chaplain at Lieber Correctional Institute where death row is located) *just left. He came this evening to see how I felt about receiving 'THE NEWS' — twenty-three days left. Yep, this afternoon the gods have ruled that my execution is set for July 1st. And so, in two days I'll be transferred to Broad River* (where the death chamber is located) *and if the lawyers stay out of it and the governor doesn't object, I will be seeing Jesus in three weeks! . . .*

'Are you ready to meet your Maker? Have you repented and accepted the Lord?' asked the padre.

I'm ready, I told him, but I haven't repented. What I did was offensive and objectionable to some folks, but I still feel that we all just about broke even. Some of the bastards got off quick and easy. Me and the ex – little misses have suffered the longest. And soon, she will win the prize for suffering the MOST – LONGEST . . . no lover, no child, no meal ticket, NO BEAUTY, NO LEGS! NO HOPE IN SHIT – ah, sweet revenge!

'Hasn't this place softened your heart, Martin? Don't ya think it's about time to forgive?'

We debated. He argued that Jesus said to turn the other cheek and that to forgive is divine and God should be the Judge. I countered that a few pages earlier God said an eye for an eye and that treason is punishable by death. I reminded him that I am a trained killer. The government taught me to kill for them. The Bible teaches that adulterers should be punished with death. (. . . nothing about co-conspirators, oh well – sucks to be them.) Hey, try solitary for about 10 years and see how forgiving ya feel . . . well – Jesus is calling in three weeks and I don't want to disappoint him. St. Peter at the pearly gates can have the last word and Satan can have my soul – I ain't changing. That's how I was taught. What did they expect?

'I ain't no saint and sure as hell ain't no savior, every other Christmas I would practice good behavior. That was then, this is now. Don't ask me to be MISTER CLEAN, cause baby I don't know how.' Allman Brothers"

Then, with one week to live:

"The madness has snuck in again, silent, insidious, gauzy, like a ghost, or vapor. One week, one week, the future inexorably washing into the present and the present, moment *by moment — without fail, without effort or thought melting into the past. I've felt it before — in the paddies, pinned down with bullets and bombs promising death if I raised my head. I felt it in residency . . . the 96 hr. Full Moon Labor Day marathon! I don't remember any sleep. I do remember the countless labor epidurals and stat C-sections, chainsaw face, no legs hobo train track sleeper — dumb ass! Tripped out motorcycle mama with the screw driver through her neck and her totally fried boy friend. And at the 94th hour — starting an emergency open heart totally bonked and no help and the surgeon screaming at everyone — "instruments, blood pressure, compressions! STOP! Who the hell are YOU? A FREAKIN' RESIDENT? Get me a real anesthesiologist NOW!" And the phone calls. The never-ending pages and calls from the ICU and OB and the OR! I can't believe that I didn't drop dead then or kill somebody after that . . . And the madness crept in again when I caught Cindy. And it flashed white hot when my baby died. I let go. Madness won. She had to pay — THEY had to pay! How much was I supposed to take? Now, MADNESS calls again. He's moved in. He is ME. I have been in this cell for too long. Too many hours, too many years, too many mind numbing, fruitless, hopeless, black days and nights. The madness is back. I am done. Finished. No more energy to fight with. No hope. No reason — just insanity. Come on shadows, ghosts, God, Jesus and take me. I am tired, just plain tired — worn out. I am already dead . . . Brutus! Bring the cup and I shall gladly drink of it."*

Two days before I met him, Martin penned:

"I wanted to write earlier today, this morning really — while it was still and quite dark in here — too dark to write. And now, I have lost some of the words, some of the thoughts and feelings but I'll try anyway. 'THE TIME' is drawing near! I meditated on IT for many hours last night. When will

IT come? How will IT feel? Who will be there? Does it matter? Not really. I am ready. The saddest and most puzzling thing is that my life had to come to this — I will end as a criminal, a monster — not a hero or a father or the kind old geezer down the block who told stories to the neighborhood kids and treated them to a popsicle when the ice cream truck made its rounds. I will not be remembered by my children, cried for at my grave or longed for after my departure. The memory of me will have no value. The memories of the few will be of unending hatred and well deserved punishment. Anyway, in the wee hours this day, I felt TIME, my time, decelerating. The spinning top of my life slowing, wobbling, tilting — no balance — scraping the bottom with a final gasp. Then silence, no motion, nothing. The end."

13

Martin's Last Words

Five months after receiving the eleven notebooks I put them down for the final time, and was glad to be finished with them.

Reading Martin's diary was like taking a ride in your brother's car with his friends — when you were nine and they were eighteen. The idea was intriguing: go to the lake on a warm summer day and jump in from the rope swing. You felt privileged to be chosen. Initially, it was enjoyable; everyone behaved, laughed and had fun.

But it wasn't long before things turned ugly; your brother veered off the pavement onto a gravel road, fishtailed to scare his friends. Then, they brought out the beer. The lake was cold, choppy and murky. Ominous clouds rolled in, threatened a murderous storm, and the rope swing terrified you. Before the day was over, the mood had turned mean, even violent. In the end, you wished you'd never agreed to be a part of the adventure.

Like the car ride, Martin's notebooks exhausted me. I don't particularly enjoy reading mean-spirited novels or watching gory movies. And I found myself all too often sympathizing with his angry feelings, especially during the darker days of my own divorce. The moment I came closest to becoming a monster myself was after the heated court battle where Kelly was awarded half of my 401K plus prorated future contributions payable as a lump sum immediately.

Later that evening, after too many beers and reading a vicious passage, I found myself perusing websites devoted to long-range sniper rifles and high-powered pistols with silencers. Martin's jailhouse writings will forever haunt me.

Martin's last words, spoken in the death chamber, have troubled me also. They've ricocheted around in my skull for all of the months that it's taken to write this book. Periodically, I have reeled from his audacity to use the Bible—God's Word—to justify, even *demand* retaliation for the sins committed against him. Yet, I will always be impressed at how rational he seemed while quoting Gibran. His voice was unwavering, even hopeful. His message was remorseless. The battle was over, and he had won. (In a few moments he would be free while Cindy would still be confined in and tortured by the prison he had built for her.)

Just as his last spoken words have plagued my brain, Martin's concluding journal entries have churned in my gut. They were written in a red-covered, two-hundred page, spiral bound notebook, but in this one Martin only filled eighty-six pages. On the inside of the front cover he had printed "THE JOURNEY HOME" in two-inch letters and blue ink. Below those words he drew a stylized sun resting on the horizon with its rays piercing a cloudless sky. The horizon was a series of jagged snow-capped mountains. In the center, the slopes of the peaks dipped down to form a deep gap from which flowed a waterway toward the viewer.

When I first saw it, I thought of the word "triumphant" for some reason. The scene was peaceful and intriguing. Did Martin title the notebook when he learned that his execution was imminent? Was the sun setting or rising? Did it signify the end of Martin's life or the dawn of a new day?

His second to last entry began: *0745 July 1, 2008.*

"This, my final morning — my last day on Earth. I awoke before the clamor of two dozen doomed men and their captors beginning their monotonous a.m. chores. I sat in the corner of this cell and thought about LIFE and the meaning of it and the END of it and what may be beyond . . . I reviewed last night's conversation with Chaplain Wilcox. We discussed (again) Cindy's treason and my reactions. Wilcox (like Marzocchi) is a good man, humble, noble. I listened then and reflected on our conversation this morning in the dark. Good and Evil. Mistakes and Forgiveness. Crime and Punishment. Heaven and Hell. Justice.

I reminded him that I had been trained to kill, a dangerous man not to be toyed with. He understood, but could not endorse it. 'We should forgive,' he said. This morning I captured those words, 'we should forgive.' I closed my eyes and boldly imprinted them on my brain. Hyperfocus. Meditate. Incorporate. Integrate. Believe! Jesus would forgive, my mother would forgive, all good people forgive. Breathe deep and listen. Forgive.

The cellblock lights flashed on. I failed."

Later that day at 1:15 p.m., Martin penned his concluding note. It was the most chilling message that I read in his journals because it was to me. Martin had plans for me, an assignment. He wrote:

"PIERRE FONTAINE! Where did you come from Pierre? At the last moment? And why? Was it cosmic curiosity? Did you simply have to meet the mad doctor? Witness with your own eyes the demon. Are you here to help me finish the mission? Will you hammer home the final nail? You're all I've got, Pierre. You're the last person that I've

met. My last hope. The Cavalry — here to complete the mission. You may be the final thought worming through my dying mind. As I float to the light. As everything fades to black — ENDS!

WHAT A LOFTY POSITION

Pierre it's all up to you. It is ALL up to you now — to expose the TRUTH — to enlighten the masses, the world. Just YOU and YOU ALONE — like JESUS or BUDDAH. YOU must unroll the scrolls and proclaim the TRUTH.

THEY WILL NOT LISTEN TO A MADMAN

But a reporter — Yes.

Tell me Pierre, am I mad? Did I overreact? Did I simply dispense justice? . . . according to the Old Testament. What would you do if someone robbed you of your LIFE? What if they stole your child, killed your child? What is the value of a life? Of what value is LIFE? What about your LIFETIME, your actual existence — all of the moments you had planned, worked, played, laughed, loved? What about your future? Those seconds, the years that were to come, moments as a family, with your child — practicing your craft . . . annihilated. Never to happen. GONE.

What would Themis place on her scales to balance a FUTURE THAT WILL NEVER HAPPEN? The culprit's life? Their future? Their joy?"

Here, Martin drew a wonderful likeness of Lady Justice holding scales. She is not blindfolded. She is glaring at the observer. A tear is falling from her right eye. The scales are perfectly balanced. On the right side, Martin printed: "MARTIN'S LIFE," on the left side he drew amputated fingers in a wheelchair, "CINDY'S JOY," and a stick figure with a hangman's noose around its neck.

"Tell me, Pierre, What would you have done? Would you have sought revenge? Could you do it? Could you penalize to the same extent as you were victimized?

'An eye for an eye!' . . . the good ole Bible.

Or, would you slink off into the faceless crowd, the spineless, the shameless cowards who've been stripped of their dignity, their worth, all hope. Would you fade away into nothingness afraid to fight back? Join the millions who have been sodomized by the SYSTEM, their lovers, the lawyers. Bullied, beaten, broken. Held Hostage. A ghost, transparent, left to wander aimlessly. Abandoned. Worthless.

Do you LIVE, Pierre? Or, are you merely alive? Are your neurons surging near capacity, buzzing, humming, electrons vaulting valences sparking the miracle of life? Once, I vaulted, burned bright, I shone like the sun . . . ELECTRIC, MAGIC, A GIANT, ALIVE! I toiled, I sweated—I became. My reward--evisceration: my heart and soul stolen. The skin you witnessed concealed a hollow core. The rotted mind you spoke with has one final act. You shall be my Joshua, your words shall be trumpets that raze the final wall and complete the destruction of the sinners.

Here are my notes, Pierre. My thoughts, my life, my soul. These pages hold your future! The secrets, the story.

A confession is what you seek isn't it, Pierre? Now, that would take all of the fun out of your investigation. A little mystery sure spices up a relationship. I've already told you about poor Thornton. His surprise! The terror in his eyes. His final gasping breath, sweet death. His blood on my hands. Of that you know I'm guilty. But where are the others?"

And with that question the diaries of Martin Cochran ended.

But his curse didn't.

Six weeks ago, after she phoned me twice, I finally sent Cindy copies of the diary as I had promised. Out of nearly seventeen hundred pages, her name only appeared in forty-two notes. In a letter that I sent to Cindy, along with the copies, I explained why there were so few pages. Unfortunately, and as I warned her, those forty-two notes were filled with hatred and evil. When I put them all together and read them, back-to-back, I shuddered to think of how she'd feel when she read them: demented, hate-filled, blood-thirsty vengeful thoughts from a sick mind. I didn't want to send them. I prayed that she could endure the pain that was sure to accompany the vile words and drawings.

As I wrapped up the first draft of this chronicle, I decided to contact Cindy Jenkins again to inform her that I would send her a copy if she liked. This way she would have an opportunity to comment on the content.

Also, I wanted to tell her that I had answered the question that her mother, my now ex-wife, and I had asked: "Why write about Martin Cochran and this whole sordid affair?" The answer, I concluded, was to expose the public to just how crazy some people can get during nasty divorces. Hopefully, from this horrid tale, couples could see the value of putting more energy into mending bruised relationships, and lawyers could learn to tone down their attacks on opposing parties. Additionally, I wanted to proudly inform Cindy that I would be donating an appreciable percentage of my profits to her directly. I wanted the funds to be available for her continued health care and living expenses.

I tried to contact her by phone but failed. I called two and three times a day and at all hours for seven days, and left messages on her machine. She never answered and I never got a reply.

Finally, after a week of calling, I listened to a recorded message that said her line had been disconnected. Then, with trepidation, I dialed her mother's number. As you can imagine, Catherine Jenkins was not happy to hear from me. And she gave me an earful.

First, when my introduction sank in, she spat out my name as if it tasted of dog shit. "Pierre Fontaine! You lousy son of a bitch! How dare you call me!" And she held her breath. I was taken aback by her vehemence and use of profanity. I steeled myself, certain that she would smash her phone hanging up. But she didn't do that immediately. She wept bitterly for a minute, and I envisioned her holding the receiver to her chest with one hand and grasping some piece of furniture with the other for balance.

"Mrs. Jenkins?" I asked hesitantly, "are you there?"

I got no answer, so I continued. "Mrs. Jenkins, I'm really sorry to bother you, but I've been trying to reach Cindy and can't. Now her phone's been disconnected, and I was hoping that you could give me her new number."

Silence, a couple of huge breaths and then an explosion. "Pierre Fontaine! You miserable bastard! Cindy is dead! Thanks to Martin Cochran and YOU!" And she slammed the receiver down.

I was flabbergasted. Cindy *dead?* And me sharing the blame with Martin?

I sat for a couple of long minutes, bewildered. How could I possibly be an accomplice in her death? Then it hit me: the diary notes. Mrs. Jenkins must think they played a part in Cindy's demise.

I knew better than to redial Cindy's mom to get the rest of the story. So, I did the next best thing: I called Lisa Stuart, Cindy's college buddy.

Ms. Stuart wasn't happy to hear from me either, but she did fill me in on what had happened to Cindy. Four weeks previous, Cindy had been hospitalized for abdominal pain. She had required surgery to fix a bowel obstruction, and was left with a colostomy. She had been more depressed than usual, and, after the operation, she was in a major funk, a black hole. Lisa said that Cindy had railed against Martin and his diary notes. And she seemed hopelessly distraught over her pitiable situation.

"She had to have a colostomy for the first six months after her attack, in order for the chemical burns on her privates to heal," Lisa said. "Now, she was told that it would have to be permanent. And Cindy said, 'Now, I'll live the rest of my life with a bag of shit on my lap!' "

"She cried and cried over that, Mr. Fontaine."

I held my breath while Lisa took a long moment and then continued.

"And then, last Monday her mother found her dead. She had taken a whole bottle of pain pills."

I almost dropped the phone. I couldn't believe what I was hearing. Cindy committed suicide.

Lisa was sniffing at this point, but composed herself enough to speak these final words before she hung up:

"She left a note . . . it said, 'HE WINS.' "

The phone went dead, and I felt my heart drain. My eyes puddled with tears. I tried to blink and sniffle them away, but couldn't. The insane bastard had won — and I'd helped. He had said, "Revenge is sweetest when served cold." And Martin had used me to get through to

Cindy one last time. After a dozen years, I had delivered the poisoned message.

I stared into space with an empty mind, but finally remembered Martin's letter to me (which I had not shared with Cindy). I had slipped it into a desk drawer all those months ago and hadn't finished reading it. Now, I wondered if the final paragraphs had held some warning, some indication of his brilliant plan, anything that could have steered me away from this project and shielded Cindy from further harm.

I remembered being frightened of the letter and only reading half of it before I had to stop. Then, I wondered if it were a Pandora's Box? If I opened it, would all of Martin's virulent, demented evils spew forth? Now, I believed that to be true. The letter contained Martin's final assault on Cindy. The evil genius recruited me into delivering his final blow. He *knew* I would write about him. He figured Cindy would read his words and relive the heinous assault, all of the terror and agony. Reading his thoughts and threats, she would re-experience his depravity and the degradation suffered at his hands. Martin hoped his diaries would send his former lover into a tailspin, hurl her deep into a vortex of inescapable miserable depression. He probably counted on her weakened condition to deteriorate. I'm certain that he hoped for her to succumb to some illness exacerbated by his planned suffocating despair.

Could he have known that she was fragile enough to take her own life? At the very least, he wanted his malevolent words to punch Cindy in the gut one last time.

As I reread the letter, I felt stupid. Martin knew how to hook me. His genius duped me into becoming an ac-

complice in his vengeful quest. He knew evil would triumph.

"*Pierre,* (the note began) *did you watch me die? Was
Cindy there? Did she cry for me . . . or for herself? Shame on
me — that wasn't nice, now was it? I have won you know.
She may have had the first laughs, some fun and games with
young Tripster, but now I am free. I have stood naked in the
wind. I have melted into the sun. My breath has been freed of
its restless tides and by now I have met God unencumbered. I
am no longer a captive. I have prevailed, the mission was a
glorious success — enemies punished, enemies vanquished.
Avenged daily, forever! Even though I am dead. Can you
imagine, Pierre?   There are things worse than death, you
know — a wheelchair or a mirror . . . Tell her I said hi and that
I have escaped my prison, my torment. My sentence was my
ticket to freedom. The good people of South Carolina have put
an end to my suffering. Pierre, talk to her for me, will you?
Tell her I'll be seeing her soon. In some strange way I do miss
her. Talk to her, Pierre, OK?"*

This is where I had put the letter down all those
months ago, but now Martin's letter went on:

"*Time is short and I can not write everything down.   I
now have 35 minutes. 35 short minutes to live. Any second
now, I will hear their voices, their foot steps — the Chaplain
reverently padding toward this cell, a guide to the after life
softly reciting incantations to his God, pleading mercy for my
soul, a witness to the demon's just reward.*
   'AN EYE FOR AN EYE'
   *Behind him — the boys — the posse, the assassins who will
chain me, propel me into the death chamber and deliver the
fatal poison.*
   AND . . . JUSTICE WILL BE SERVED

But, whose Justice, Pierre? The State's Justice, God's Justice, Cosmic Justice, Blind Justice? God's Justice is either an eye for an eye or turn the other cheek depending on which page you turn to. (What's your agenda?) . . . Cosmicly — what goes around — you know . . . huh Cindy? . . . and Blind Justice — absolute impartiality, what's that?   Justice, my friend, is simply a sanctioned form of revenge.

So what about some Justice for Martin?

Take the Scales, Pierre. Hold them in your hands. Measure my losses against Cindy's treason. Do they balance? I think not.

You hold the scales Pierre and put a final little pinch of pain on her side for me. OK?

Anyway, Pierre, enough of that. Think about this. This is some wild shit: THE STATE'S JUSTICE will, in a very few minutes, direct and conduct a premeditated murder. MY MURDER! Years ago, THE STATE trained and paid me to kill those deemed a threat to THE STATE'S wellbeing. What about my wellbeing? THE STATE forbids killing humans, yet is going to kill me for killing Thornton. Hmm.

I know what this day holds for me, THE END.

What will those last seconds feel like, Pierre? Those final moments of my existence. The same ride that Thornton took. Less messy I hope. Poisons scalding my veins, breath faltering, the ceiling fading to black, asystole. Nothing.

But does 'IT' stop when I cease? Do I then step onto those scales, face GOD, transmute into the verdict. What of ETERNITY Pierre?

Hey! I hear them coming Pierre — one last thing!

On this, the final morning of my life, 12 hours before my scheduled murder, I deliberated — CRIME and PUNISHMENT — the events that led me to this black moment. I repaid my suffering with suffering.

213

AN EYE FOR AN EYE

I listened to the voices of the Universe all those years ago — Deus et Satanas — and followed orders. This morning, I cleared my mind and I heard those words again. They are my final words to you — to Cindy — to the world.

The Angel on my right shoulder virtuously chastised, 'Martin, it was not your place to judge or repay. Vengeance is mine says the Lord.'

But the devil on my left viciously struck back,

"Yeah, but NEVER fuck with a Marine!"

Epilogue

I'm not certain that I could have interpreted Martin's coded message in advance of Cindy's death, but, in retrospect, it's clear to me that he wanted to wound Cindy one last time. His final written words shouted a warning to all: "I'm a dangerous man, not to be toyed with." And he made it plain that he'd follow the path of vengeance when he trumpeted the black angel's warning to never mess with a Marine. His deathbed words left no doubt that he believed Cindy should be held to Old Testament justice: death.

As I've thought about the ending of this story, I've wondered if the journal notes describing his jungle experiences were clues to his plan to use prolonged torture ending in Cindy's eventual death. Hard to say.

My plans to help Cindy financially are now moot. Instead I've decided to donate the same amount of funds to survivors of domestic abuse. Also, I've begun to see a psychologist in order to work through feelings of guilt relating to Cindy's death, feelings of being duped by Martin, being an accomplice, and to work through my anger issues with Kelly. I've been advised to, "Let it go. Change the 'Now and the Future.' You are powerless to change the past."

I'm trying to follow that advice. Also, I'm taking a suggestion from my ex-wife: I've begun working on a new tale. It's the story of Emma Corn, a beautiful Southern woman who survived the racial trials of the Twentieth Century and championed those of lesser fortune. Emma Corn was a hero. Her story is helping me be a better person.

About the Author

Michael Landolfi loves to tell a story. He says his first one goes like this: In 1959, when he was two years old, he grew weary of Atlanta. So, he packed a few things and moved his parents to Asheville, where he has spent most of his life.

He survived Catholic grade school, attended a few weeks of high school and spent three years in the Marine Corps. In 1982, he earned a Bachelor of Science in Nursing and added a Master's Degree in Nurse Anesthesia in 1998. He's provided health care and anesthesia services in hospitals all over the country. And during breaks in the action, he's fascinated audiences with wild tales of his mischievous youth and near-death outdoor escapades.

He's still climbing rock walls and frozen waterfalls, peddling roads and trails, solo backpacking to remote mountaintops in stupid weather and he's close to figuring out the relationship between time, gravity and quantum mechanics.

Check out his other two books: *5-Minute Short Stories - A Bathroom Book* and *5- Minute Short Stories - Another Bathroom Book.*